He placed the blanket around her shoulders and adjusted it so that it covered all of her. But he lingered. And his fingers brushed over her collarbone, inciting another shiver that had nothing to do with the weather.

Sawyer must have noticed and his eyes focused on her lips. Before she could protest, he was tugging the blanket toward him, which had the added effect of bringing her right to him. Riley raised her head. Big mistake. It only put his sumptuous mouth in front of her.

How could she resist?

They stood like that for a moment. A long, heated moment. She didn't know who moved first. Maybe they both did. She let out a gasp and then once again, their lips met.

Who knew Sawyer Wallace could kiss like this? If he wasn't holding her up by the blanket, her knees would have given out.

After what felt like hours, they parted. Gently, he kissed the tip of her nose before pulling her in for a long hug.

"Riley, that was—"

"Something that absolutely cannot happen again," she finished sadly.

*

SAVED BY THE BLO
gossip columnist won't

Dear Reader,

I can't believe it! We're already at the final book in the Saved by the Blog series! Seems like I just started writing it yesterday.

I was so excited to get to this book because I couldn't wait to write about Riley Hudson. Describing her outfits alone was so much fun. But under the fabulous wardrobe and coordinating accessories, Riley has some secrets. The biggest of which is a fear of getting hurt...again. Perhaps her best friend and boss, Sawyer Wallace, will discover the way to Riley's heart!

The other big news in this book is the revelation of the Bayside Blogger. Have you guessed who it is? As the Bayside Blogger would say, *You'll have to read to find out because I'll never tell. Smirk.*

Bayside is not the only small town in my life. You may have noticed the dedication of this book is to my hometown of Monessen. Even though I no longer live there, the support and love I've received from everyone there has been overwhelming. Thank you, Greyhounds!

So that's it for now. But don't worry. I'll be back with more books soon. I'm hard at work on a new wedding-themed miniseries featuring a group of friends who... Well, I won't spoil it for you. [emoji: winking happy face]

In the meantime, I want to give a big shout-out and thank-you to my fabulous editor, Susan Litman. I love working with you and love talking about *The Walking Dead* even more. Thank you to everyone at Harlequin for making my dreams a reality and being so fabulous to work with.

I hope you enjoyed the entire Saved by the Blog series. I'd love to connect, so please visit my website at kerricarpenter.com or find me on Facebook, Twitter and Instagram as AuthorKerri.

Happy reading and glitter toss,

Kerri Carpenter

Bayside's Most Unexpected Bride

———

Kerri Carpenter

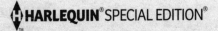

HARLEQUIN® SPECIAL EDITION®

Recycling programs
for this product may
not exist in your area.

ISBN-13: 978-1-335-46553-5

Bayside's Most Unexpected Bride

Copyright © 2017 by Kerri Carpenter

Printed in U.S.A.

www.Harlequin.com

Award-winning romance author **Kerri Carpenter** writes contemporary romances that are sweet, sexy and sparkly. When she's not writing, Kerri enjoys reading, cooking, watching movies, taking Zumba classes, rooting for Pittsburgh sports teams and anything sparkly. Kerri lives in Northern Virginia with her adorable (and mischievous) rescued poodle mix, Harry. Visit Kerri at her website, kerricarpenter.com, on Facebook (Facebook.com/AuthorKerri,) Twitter and Instagram (@authorkerri), or subscribe to her newsletter.

For my very own small town,
the place that made me who I am today.
To my hometown of Monessen and
all of those fellow Greyhounds
who have been supporting me since day one.

Chapter One

It's beginning to look a lot like Christmas... Well, kind of. Thanksgiving is right around the corner and before we know it, the Yuletide season will be here. Looks like everyone's favorite editor in chief is starting the festivities early by spending time with local hottie Holly Carron. The duo were spotted at The Brewside yesterday looking quite cozy. And right when everyone thought Bayside's forever bachelor would never settle down! Stay tuned for more developing details...

Riley studied the screen in front of her and pursed her lips. Yep, Sawyer was going to be pissed. *The Bayside Blogger strikes again.* He hated when she wrote about him.

Who didn't?

Riley fluffed her red hair, held back with an oversize blue headband to complement her green-and-blue-plaid dress with the adorable white collar. She'd seen this dress in the store and knew instantly that she could rock the retro vibe. What would the ubiquitous Bayside Blogger say about her outfit? Riley grinned. She knew exactly what she'd say.

Everyone's favorite ex-Manhattanite Riley Hudson is sporting her wannabe New York fashion in small-town Virginia. Hard to be fashion forward when she's just copying Kim Kardashian's recent ensemble. Always the bridesmaid, Riley.

"Hey, Ri, did you file that article on the upcoming holiday movies?"

Riley glanced up to see her coworker Claudia Thomas hovering above her cubicle. Claudia was the most striking woman Riley had ever seen, with her long, jet-black hair, delicate features and statuesque six-foot height. Definitely didn't fit into their quaint coastal town on the Chesapeake Bay. She was also the senior editor in the Style & Entertainment section, which Riley wrote for.

"Yep, just sent it your way. I think I covered the majority of the new ones, plus I added my top-ten holiday classics. Got a couple good quotes from the guys over at the Palace Movie Theater, too."

"Excellent," Claudia said with a big smile. She spotted Riley's computer screen and gestured toward it. "I see you're reading the Bayside Blogger's column today. Sawyer is gonna be *pissed*."

"Uh, yeah, just finished it. But I don't know why he would be. A ton of people saw him at The Brewside with Holly yesterday."

Claudia leaned onto the wall of Riley's cubicle. "But you know how he hates to be featured in that column. The Bayside Blogger should really tread lightly, especially since Sawyer is the only person who knows her identity."

Riley fidgeted in her chair. "It's not like he would out her. Or him. Not after all this time."

"Maybe not." Claudia lowered her voice conspiratorially. "You think it's serious with him and Holly?"

Riley suddenly felt uncomfortable. She shrugged. "Who knows?"

Sawyer Wallace was more than the editor in chief and owner of the *Bayside Bugle*. More than her boss.

She'd known him her entire life. Two years older than her, their families were very close and had always shared holidays, vacations, barbecues and practically every important milestone.

Sawyer was like an annoying older brother, only... not brotherly at all.

"My friend Vivica asked him out a couple weeks ago."

Riley perked up at that tidbit. She straightened in her chair. "Really? I didn't know that."

"Probably because Sawyer turned her down. Crazy, because Vivica is the most gorgeous woman I've ever seen. But, personally, I think something's going on with him."

They both turned toward the glass office in the corner of the newsroom where Sawyer was intently studying his computer screen.

"Something bad?" Riley asked.

"You tell me. Your families are tight."

Riley eyed Sawyer in his office again. Apparently not that tight. Although, he had been extra surly lately. Sawyer did that whole stereotypical moody-writer thing well. But it never bothered her. In fact, she always knew how to make him lighten up and laugh.

"I say we get him drunk at this year's holiday party and force him to reveal the identity of the Bayside Blogger," Claudia said.

Riley smiled. "I don't think there's enough spiked eggnog on the planet to get that closely guarded secret out of him. Besides, I've tried."

Everyone in town had tried at one point or another. The Bayside Blogger not only had a daily column in *The Bayside Bugle*, but she—or he—also had a blog and utilized every social media channel imaginable. No one was off-limits—the blogger always seemed to know every-thing about everyone, anytime, anywhere.

"I can't believe he won't tell anyone who she is. Even us. We work here, for goodness sake. And that damn Blogger is published in my section."

"We should go on strike," Riley stated dramatically, making Claudia laugh.

"You may be onto something. In the meantime, I'm going to read over your article. Oh, by the way, my hus-band and I are going to take a weekend trip to New York in December. You know, see the holiday windows and the big tree and Rockefeller Center."

Riley tensed. "Cool."

"I know you lived there for a while. Maybe you can give us some restaurant recommendations."

She twisted her fingers together. "Well, you know New York. Everything's constantly changing. I haven't been back in a couple years. I'm totally out of touch."

But she wasn't. After graduating from Syracuse, Riley had moved to the city that never sleeps. She'd worked at a start-up marketing firm writing copy and social media posts. She'd lived in a massively overpriced studio apart-ment where she'd had to store her shoes in her oven and hang her laundry from her curtain rods.

It had been fabulous. Everything she'd always wanted. Living in the greatest city in the world. She'd stayed out late and seen Broadway shows and walked down Fifth Avenue at night. As often as her entry-level salary al-lowed, she'd tried new restaurants and bakeries. She'd been dazzled by the lights, the sounds, the people.

At least, that's what she let people think of her expe-rience in the Big Apple. It was easier to pretend her life was closer to *Friends* than *Two Broke Girls*.

When she'd returned to Bayside for holidays, she'd

never been able to let the truth slip, which was that pretending to be a sophisticated young twentysomething in Manhattan was exhausting. And frustrating. And expensive. And…disappointing.

She'd wanted to live in Manhattan forever. She'd had a whole picture of what her life would be like, but the reality never matched up to it.

She was supposed to have an amazing job, a large apartment with tall windows that overlooked Central Park, a group of friends to rival Monica, Rachel and Phoebe. And, of course, her cool boyfriend would be the icing on the cupcake.

But that's not how Connor McKenzie turned out to be.

She frowned. She'd seen no harm in dating her coworker. After all, their company hadn't had a policy against it. At least, that's what he'd told her. Why wouldn't little old naive twenty-two-year-old Riley believe the dazzling, successful thirty-year-old Connor?

So, all had been well…until it wasn't. She'd moved back home.

Well, more like run back with her tail between her legs. Now she never talked about her time in Manhattan if she could help it. Or she'd tell people the version she knew they expected to hear. At twenty-nine, Riley had definitely learned her lesson.

Claudia's face fell and Riley relented. She hated letting anyone down. "I mean, I guess I could put a list together. Remind me."

This seemed to appease Claudia. "Great. And don't forget, editorial meeting this afternoon."

"Wouldn't miss it."

Riley watched her editor walk to her office before returning to her screen and studying Sawyer's name embedded in the Bayside Blogger's column. Maybe Claudia was wrong. Maybe he wouldn't get too mad about it.

"Hudson." Sawyer's voice boomed out from his office. "Get in here."

As she got up and adjusted her dress, more than one head turned in her direction with sympathetic eyes. Never a good thing when Sawyer used his outdoor voice. Or called her by her last name.

"What's with him?" Dennis, her next-door cubicle mate, asked quietly.

"Dunno. Probably pissed about that restaurant review I did. They were an advertiser."

"Hold strong." He touched his stomach. "I ate there, too. It wasn't good."

Riley grabbed her notebook and pen. "Will do." Then she headed toward Sawyer with the sinking feeling she already knew what this was about.

When she reached his office, she stayed where she was in the doorway. She crossed her legs, accentuating the fabulous brown suede knee-high boots she'd bought in DC last weekend when she and her best friend, Elle, had driven to the city for a girls' weekend.

"Hey, boss. What's up?"

He steepled his hands on his desk and peered at her with his dreamy hazel eyes.

Damn. *Dreamy?* She meant *irritating. Beady* even.

The weather was unseasonably cold already and he was sporting a pair of corduroy pants and a somewhat ugly argyle sweater that she knew had been a Christmas gift from his mother last year. Not the most stylish of outfits and yet somehow he looked like he'd walked out of the pages of an L.L.Bean catalog. Just because he was tall with broad shoulders and had really cute sandy-brown hair that flopped on his head because he needed a haircut. And today he was wearing his glasses. What was it about a large lumberjack-looking man who wore glasses? Why did that make her stomach twist up into knots? And then there was his lopsided smile…

What in the heck was she doing? This was Sawyer Wallace, lifelong friend and, more importantly, boss. She couldn't size him up like a piece of meat. Especially because they worked together. Especially because of what had happened to her in New York.

"Riley," he began.

"Sawyer," she countered, and bit her lip in anticipation.

He reached into his top desk drawer and pulled out a colorful silk scarf. "Before I forget, Tony found this at The Brewside. Said you left it there a couple of weeks ago and he kept forgetting to give it to you."

She reached for the bright yellow scarf with lime-green polka dots. One of her favorites.

"Thanks," she mumbled. "Tony must have given this to you while you were on your date." She used air quotes for the word *date* and wiggled her eyebrows.

Sawyer exhaled a long breath.

"What?" she asked, feigning innocence.

"'Bayside's forever bachelor'?" he quoted. "Really?"

She shrugged.

"I thought I told you to keep me out of the Bayside Blogger's column."

Riley stepped into his office and closed the door. She didn't sit in either of the chairs in front of the ancient oak desk in his office. The desk that had belonged to his great-great-grandfather. Instead, she remained standing in front of him, wearing a sexy little dress that looked like something he'd once seen on a rerun of *The Mary*

Tyler Moore Show. Not to mention those boots that show-cased her shapely legs.

She was wringing her hands, he noticed. That meant she'd already realized he wasn't going to like being an item in her gossip column.

"You wrote about me? Seriously?"

Riley scrunched up her nose in a way he found distracting. And...cute. "I've written about you before. Besides, it wouldn't be fair to exclude you just because you work at the *Bugle*."

He arched a brow. "Because I own the *Bugle*, you mean?"

"Well, no one's off-limits. That was the deal we made when I started doing this."

"I know. Believe me, I know." Did he ever. When Riley had originally pitched him the idea of a gossip column he'd had no idea what the Bayside Blogger would become. He'd only said yes because she'd been so excited about it.

After she'd returned from New York City, the usually bubbly girl he'd known forever had been different. Somber, quiet, less bubbly. Not for the first time, Sawyer wondered what exactly had happened to her in Manhattan. But she never talked about it and changed the subject if New York was even brought up.

His phone chirped and he saw a text message from his mother. He gestured to his phone. "Do you see this? You have my mom reading your column."

"I love your mom. Tell her I said hi."

Sawyer gritted his teeth. "My mom follows the Bayside Blogger. My mom mentioned the article and I told her it wasn't true. She just asked me via text if I was planning to propose to Holly and when I said no, she asked if I was gay."

"Fair question," she said with a wry smile.

He nailed her with a hard stare. Riley remained completely unaffected. They'd known each other too long for intimidation. Hell, they'd known each other their entire lives. Of course, that's what happened when you grew up in a small coastal town like Bayside, Virginia.

"You know I'm not gay."

Her gaze ran over him. "Of course you're not gay. Look at that outfit."

"Cute."

"Thanks." She plopped down in a chair. "Honestly, I don't know what you're upset about. I didn't write anything that bad."

He leaned toward her. "You said I was on a date."

"I had multiple sources email and direct message me on Twitter about your little daytime rendezvous."

Sawyer knew Riley got tips all day long from her many sources. For, as much as they complained, the residents of Bayside couldn't keep themselves from joining the gossip train. They apparently loved helping the Bayside Blogger report on one another. They emailed her directly or through the *Bugle*'s website and left Facebook and Twitter messages. Last summer Riley had been able to take a weeklong vacation without the gossip stopping.

He'd claim the whole thing was preposterous, but the numbers didn't lie. The gossip column was the most viewed area of the online edition of the paper. He couldn't help but wonder what his ancestors who'd started the newspaper would think of that.

Still, he wasn't letting her off the hook that easily. "You know I wasn't on a date with Holly."

She raised her nose in a regal gesture. "I know nothing of the kind."

"She's one of our best freelance photographers. We

were meeting about an assignment." Even he could hear the defensiveness in his voice. And why did he feel the need to explain himself to Riley?

"You could've met here at the office."

"I needed caffeine." And he'd needed to get away for a little bit.

Running a daily newspaper wasn't the easiest of jobs these days. Not that it ever had been. Balancing editorial with the business side, advertisers and marketing. Not to mention the dwindling circulation numbers.

He really wished he didn't have to mention that.

"Is the *Bugle* in trouble?"

Damn, she was the most perceptive person he'd ever met. Probably why she was so good at being the Bayside Blogger.

He noticed the concern on her face. It probably mirrored his own. Still, he didn't want to worry her or anyone on staff. So far he'd been able to keep all of the financial concerns to himself. "No more than every other paper in the country."

"Maybe you could raise the price. I'm sure people would pay…"

He shook his head as she trailed off. "You know that circulation doesn't keep newspapers afloat. Advertisers do."

A small line formed on her forehead as she considered that. "But you said that advertisers have been fighting to get in."

"Just in your section." Which was true. Everyone wanted to appear in the Bayside Blogger's section since they knew that everyone in town was reading the gossip. Bayside had its fair share of restaurants and local businesses, but a small town offered only so many resources.

And without more advertising, they'd be closing up shop by the end of the next summer season.

The truth was, Riley's question was on target. The *Bugle* was in trouble. Sawyer had tried to stay on top of it by utilizing their website and digital edition and making sure the design was up-to-date. He'd even downsized the print edition to cut costs at every corner.

But now he had some tough decisions to make, the biggest being layoffs. He was already running with a skeleton crew in the advertising department. He hated to think about shrinking the editorial team. He swiped a hand over his face. Employee layoffs at Christmastime. Could there be anything worse?

"Sawyer, are you okay? What's going on?"

Riley's voice pulled him out of his funk even though he knew he was going to have to deal with it soon. In the meantime, he'd explore all options and do everything in his power to not have to fire anyone. At Christmas or any other time. And he'd definitely work hard to keep this from his team. Even if it meant not drawing his own salary.

"Nothing is going on and I'm fine. Stop worrying. On to other business. The upcoming Christmas Kickoff Festival."

Riley eyed him skeptically for another moment before flipping open her reporter's notebook. "Day after Thanksgiving, just like always."

"With a twist," Sawyer interjected. "Usually, this is a townie thing. But I was at the council meeting the other night. They want to go big, attract people from other towns and areas of Virginia."

"Impressive."

"They want it to be a smaller version of New York's lighting of the Rockefeller Center tree."

He noticed her pen skip at the mention of New York. "I want you to cover the event. This is right up your alley. Plus, you lived there, so you'd have the experience of knowing what their ceremony is like."

"I never went to the tree lighting when I lived there," she said in a soft voice.

Sawyer knew that wasn't true. Riley had lived in New York for four years. During that time, she'd always been active on social media, and he remembered seeing her Facebook pictures of tree lightings over the years. But, once again, she didn't want to talk about New York. So, once again, he would let it go. For now.

"Still, I'd like you to head up the festival for the *Bugle*. Let's start getting some pre-event coverage in both the print and online editions."

Now she was scribbling in her notebook. Concentrating. Looking sexy as hell.

Get a grip, Wallace.

"Oh, I wanted to ask you about that recent social media promotion you and Claudia ran. Why were the numbers so low?"

Her gaze flicked up quickly to his. Her eyes narrowed. "The numbers were fine. Normal."

"Not from the report you sent me. The reach was lower than the last contest."

She gifted him with an overdramatic sigh. "How many times do I have to explain social media to you?"

The side of his mouth twitched but he held in the smile. One of his favorite things about Riley was how bright she was. Most people didn't realize that under her coordinated outfits and talk of the latest docudrama airing on Bravo, Riley had a shrewd eye for social media, pop culture and how to use those things in business.

"Humor me," he told her.

"You were looking at the total reach of the posts on all the platforms. Did you check the organic reach? The numbers were fabulous, especially considering how you cut our social media advertising budget to shreds."

"I don't see how that—"

She continued on her rant and Sawyer couldn't follow it, although, he was impressed as hell. He might not understand a lick of what she was saying, but he really loved watching how passionate she became as she explained it.

"Are you listening to me?"

Her question jerked him away from his thoughts. He decided that talking to Riley about social media wasn't going to help anything. Especially because he didn't want to reveal that she was going to have even less money in the budget next year.

"What are you up to this weekend?" he asked.

If his change in topic came as a surprise to her, she didn't show it. "Same as you," she said with a bemused smile. He racked his brain and couldn't think of any shared family gatherings until Thanksgiving. Riley rolled her eyes. "Tomorrow is Elle and Cam's engagement party at the Dumont estate. There's no way you could have forgotten that."

His turn to roll his eyes. "Blocked, perhaps."

"Sawyer, it's not that bad. Most people love when the Dumonts throw parties."

"Which is practically every week."

The Dumont family had also been in Bayside for generations. They owned Dumont Incorporated, headed up by Jasper Dumont now. Jasper was Cam's brother and Sawyer was close with both of them. He was happy his friend had popped the question to Elle. Thrilled to celebrate with them. What he didn't particularly look forward to was dressing in a monkey suit and mingling with most of the town at yet another black-tie party.

He saw the excitement on Riley's face, though. This kind of event was much more her thing. She was so good at socializing and enjoying large crowds. Not to mention, she looked damn fine in a gown.

"Come on," she cooed. "There has to be something about tomorrow's party you can look forward to."

An image of her in a tight black dress from the last Dumont soiree flitted into his mind. All of that amazing red hair had been piled in curls atop her head. Her shoulders had been bare and she'd worn the sexiest pair of stilettos… His mouth went dry thinking about it.

He almost jerked backward. What in the heck was he doing? He couldn't think about Riley like that. He could still remember the doll she used to carry around when they were kids.

"Earth to Sawyer," she said impatiently.

"There's always the free alcohol," he covered.

Oblivious to his thoughts, she nodded. "There you go. Now, you just have to get your date Holly on board."

He gritted his teeth. "I am not dating Holly."

"I wouldn't care if you were." Her eyes narrowed as she considered. "Are you bringing anyone else tomorrow? Like, as a date?"

He shook his head. "Nope. You?" He held his breath.

"No. It's hard to be Riley Hudson, the Bayside Blogger, and enjoy being on a date. You know that."

He did. She committed her life to the *Bugle*, sacrificing much of her social life to write the column that was keeping the paper in the black—barely. He opened his mouth to thank her, but the words caught in his throat. The sun was slanting through the blinds, highlighting her coppery hair, the freckles on her ivory nose, that amazing body.

Had she always been this beautiful? Why was he only noticing her now, when he couldn't possibly make a move?

Ah, heck. He was feeling something for his lifelong friend that he had no business feeling.

She stood to leave but hesitated next to her chair. "Sawyer, are you sure you're okay?"

"Uh, yeah, I'm fine."

She reached for the door but turned back again. "And the *Bugle* is fine, too? It's not in any trouble?"

Her hand was on her hip, accentuating the fact that even for a petite woman she had curves. He swallowed hard. "Don't worry, Riley. Everything will be fine."

Sawyer wasn't entirely sure if she believed him. She lingered a moment more before departing.

He felt bad about lying to his oldest friend, saying the *Bugle* wasn't in trouble. But it sure was—and so was he.

Chapter Two

Who's excited for tonight's party at the Dumonts'? I can't think of a better way to ring in the holiday season than champagne and dancing with a view of the bay! And you just never know who might show up at a Dumont affair, so this blogger is keeping her eyes open, Baysiders!

Riley crossed the terrace and took in the sight of the Dumont estate in full party mode. A cold breeze caused goose bumps to rise on her skin, hardly surprising since it was almost Thanksgiving. Not to mention that Riley was wearing nothing more than a gown and a thin wrap. Still, she couldn't help but take a moment to soak in her surroundings.

With its cascading terraces and gorgeous grounds, this was so much more than a house. It was like something out of an old black-and-white movie. With tennis courts and swimming pools, even an atrium, the Dumont mansion sat right on the bay, surrounded by strategically placed fences and bushes for privacy.

Riley made her way into the large heated tent set up on the lower grounds. Several bars occupied the corners of the space, while waiters flitted throughout the crowd of black tie–bedecked guests listening to a large band seated on a raised platform. Crystal chandeliers hung from the ceiling and tasteful twinkly lights were strung from one corner to another. And then there were the candles. Riley had never seen so many in one place. Mrs. Dumont had gone above and beyond tonight.

All Dumont parties were special, but this one was extra special. Cameron, the oldest Dumont brother, had recently popped the question to Elle Owens, one of Riley's two best friends. Everyone in town was thrilled to see the two of them together, but Riley in particular. She liked to think the Bayside Blogger had had a hand in their relationship. Sometimes people just needed a push.

And speaking of pushes…

Riley did a quick glance around the tent, taking in all the players. She had a keen memory, which came in handy for recalling details when she wrote her column.

She snagged a glass of champagne from a passing waiter as she continued surveying the party. A handful of people were already dancing, but mostly there was a lot of chatting over appetizers. And…she grinned. Over in the corner she saw Simone Graves getting her flirt on with Sam Roberts, who'd just taken a job at the high school. Interesting. She whipped her cell phone out and quickly made a note.

"What's that sly smile for?"

Riley looked up to see her other best friend, Carissa Blackwell, smirking back at her. "Look at you, gorgeous," Riley said, instead of answering the question.

"You like?"

Carissa was wearing a navy blue floor-length dress. Her blond hair was piled on top of her head and her makeup was flawless. She was tall and curvy with the most beautiful gray eyes. If they weren't friends, Riley would hate her on principle.

"Stunning," Riley replied. "I can see the drool on Jasper's chin from here." She waved at Jasper, who was all the way on the other side of the tent. He'd been beaming with adoration at his girlfriend the whole time. Carissa turned and winked at him.

It was official. Both Dumont brothers were off the market. Too bad for Bayside's singletons, but hooray for her friends. She couldn't be happier they'd found their soul mates.

She sighed. Well…mostly happy. Totally happy, she amended quickly. She was thrilled for Carissa and Elle. It was just that it would be kind of nice to find someone for herself.

Of course, last time she'd had a serious boyfriend it hadn't turned out so great. Maybe she should watch what she wished for.

"Riley!"

She shook her head and tuned back into Carissa, who was standing with her hands on her hips, an expectant look on her face.

"Sorry, what?" Riley asked.

Carissa narrowed her eyes. "I said, you look great, too."

Riley was wearing a new curve-hugging, low-backed dress in her favorite color, emerald green. She'd put her hair up in a messy yet chic ponytail, leaving wild strands loose around her face.

"Oh well, thank you. And speaking of looking good…" She wiggled her eyebrows as Elle, the bride-to-be, sidled up to them.

"You look very bridal," Riley said, gesturing to Elle's off-white gown. Of course, she'd helped her pick out the dress a month ago. "Practicing for the big day already?"

"Don't mention the big day. I'm stressed." She grabbed a champagne flute from a passing waiter.

"Oh no," Riley said. "What can we do?"

"Are you kidding? You've both been bridesmaids of the year so far. Between you two, my soon-to-be mother-in-law, every bridal magazine ever written, and even my dad, I think I may be approaching too much help."

"Too many opinions?" Carissa guessed.

Elle grimaced. "Too many *very* strong opinions."

As they chatted about the upcoming spring wedding a little longer, Riley couldn't help noticing that something was off with Carissa.

"What?" Riley asked.

"What do you mean what?" Carissa countered.

Riley wiggled her pointer finger in front of Carissa. "Something's up. I can tell."

Carissa turned to Elle. "I swear, she's a psychic or something."

"It is eerie sometimes," Elle agreed. "But is something wrong, Car? You look a little pale."

"No, not wrong. The opposite of wrong, actually. Just scary."

"Can you be a little more cryptic?" Riley laughed.

"Sorry." Carissa glanced across the tent. Riley followed her gaze and saw that Jasper was deep in conversation with his brother. "Jasper asked me to move in with him this morning."

"Whoa, that's huge."

Riley wondered if the Bayside Blogger should mention this. She chewed on her lip as she considered. It was pretty major news. Carissa and Jasper had been hot and heavy back in high school. Then they'd broken up right after graduation and hadn't seen each other for years. After Carissa's divorce, she'd moved back to Bayside to start her catering business, Save the Day Catering, which had really taken off. She'd not only gotten back together with Jasper, but they would be opening a bookstore and café soon. And now they were taking the next step. Cohabitation.

All of this was right up the Bayside Blogger's alley, but Riley knew that her friends—just like Sawyer—hated being written about. Still, she couldn't leave them out of the column. She'd become tight with Elle and Car. Everyone in town knew that. If she didn't mention them from time to time, then her identity would be obvious.

Maybe she should wait a couple days and see how this played out.

"There's more," Carissa said, drawing Riley and Elle's attention. "A lot more."

Riley immediately let her gaze drop to Carissa's ring finger. The all-important finger was empty of a ring.

"What's going on?" Riley asked.

"Well, um, I went to the doctor yesterday."

Elle's face washed of color. Her father had dealt with bladder cancer recently and Elle was particularly sensitive to talk of doctors. "You weren't feeling well a couple days ago. I remember. You had to run out of our brunch when you got sick."

"Right," Carissa said.

Elle grabbed one of Carissa's hands. Riley took the other.

"Are you okay?" Riley asked, her pulse skyrocketing.

"Well, turns out I'm…pregnant."

A long moment of astonished silence passed between them. Riley didn't know who started it, but then all three of them were screaming and hugging.

"Ohmigod, ohmigod, ohmigod. How did this happen?" Riley asked. "I mean, I know how it happens."

Carissa laughed. "We've always been so careful. Except, well, this one time."

Elle hugged Carissa again. "And one time is all it takes. Congratulations."

"Thank you. I wasn't going to tell anyone yet, but I just couldn't keep it from you two. So mum's the word until I say. Especially from the men."

They agreed and hugged some more.

"Speaking of men," Carissa began as she pinned Riley with a knowing glare.

Uh-oh. She had a feeling what was coming even though they weren't talking about men. "Don't start, Car," Riley begged.

"I'm just saying. When was the last time you went on a date?"

Riley shook her head. "I'm focusing on my career right now." Which was a total lie. Elle saw through it immediately.

"You were just saying the other day how you could do your job with your eyes closed." Elle wagged a finger at her. "I know for a fact that Jason Wellington asked you out last week and you blew him off. What gives?"

Riley opened her mouth to answer, but the words caught in her throat as she noticed Sawyer walk into the tent. Her mouth went dry at the sight of him in his tux, which was stupid really because she'd seen him in a tuxedo before. Many times. She supposed it had to do with the fact that he usually wore jeans and… Wow, he'd shaved today instead of leaving his face all scruffy. Although, normally, his scruff was appealing too.

What was she doing? What was she thinking? This was Sawyer. She'd known him her whole life. She couldn't get all swoony over him. Only he'd just noticed her, too. He grinned and she felt like someone had punched her in the stomach.

He started to walk toward her and once again her

friends faded away. Her knees actually went weak like she was one of the characters in those Hallmark Channel movies she loved so much.

Only this wasn't a movie. The way her heart started racing was very, very real.

Riley always looked amazing. But tonight? For an editor, a man who dealt with every aspect of a newspaper every single day, he had no words.

At first, he'd thought the green dress was a bit demure for her. Then she'd turned around—the back of it was close to nonexistent. It dipped low, almost to her shapely behind.

Again he chastised himself. He wasn't supposed to be thinking about her behind. Or her front. He shook his head. Or any side of her. Except the friend side. They'd practically grown up as siblings. No, that wasn't quite right.

He should stop walking toward her, yet he couldn't. He noticed she wore dangly earrings that sparkled so brightly they practically lit up the whole tent on their own. Very Riley-esque. Because when he thought about her, he thought about a bright light.

When he reached her, she smiled, but otherwise stayed silent. He turned to Elle and Carissa, who were both wearing the oddest expressions. They exchanged mysterious looks with one another.

"Congrats again, Elle," he offered. "I'm thrilled for you and Cam."

"Thanks, Sawyer. Have you said hi to Cam yet?"

"Uh, no, I just got here."

"And came right over to us," Carissa said. Then she exchanged a second look with Elle, who bit down on her lip like she was trying to keep from laughing.

Women were enigmatic to him sometimes.

"Well, I really must find my fiancé," Elle said.

Carissa jumped slightly. "Yes, and I need to find Jasper and check with my assistant. Save the Day catered tonight's soiree, so I expect you all to make copious yummy noises throughout the party."

Sawyer laughed as Elle and Carissa said their goodbyes and disappeared into the crowd. He turned to Riley.

"Hey," he said lamely.

"Hey you," she replied. "You look…" She trailed off and tilted her head. Then she reached forward and fiddled with his tie. "There. It was crooked."

"Thanks." The word lingered on his lips the same way her hand lingered on his chest. He could smell her perfume. He didn't know what it was, but it smelled amazing, like flowers dipped in more flowers.

"Quite the dress, Ri," he said when she finally took a step back. "You should consider yourself lucky that your dad is out of town or he would have thrown his coat over you and hauled you out of here."

She waved him away. "Oh, please. It's not that bad."

To prove her point, she did a little spin. His mouth went dry at seeing all that silky skin up close. Not to mention he couldn't help but realize she couldn't wear a bra. Suddenly his tie felt incredibly restrictive.

He tried to make light of the situation. "If I remember correctly, you always did give your parents a run for their money with your various fashion choices."

Again she waved her hand. "Experimenting with outfits and accessories is part of finding yourself."

"And I imagine all those times you came home late from dates was also some sort of experimenting? Now that I think about it, you were a bit of a wild child, Riley Hudson."

"Hardly. I think I was a fairly normal teenager. And anyway, easy for you to say. You've always been Mr. Dependable, son of the year."

He didn't have to see himself in a mirror to know his face fell. "Not always, Ri."

Sawyer really didn't know why he was goading her. He'd been called into the principal's office more than he should ever admit. Wasn't his fault he'd had a penchant for pranks.

Of course, that was all child's play compared to his antics after he'd graduated from college. He'd been in love and like many young people in love, he'd made Rachel his whole life.

Unfortunately, it had taken him a couple years to realize that Rachel wasn't the right fit. In fact, some might call them polar opposites.

But he'd been besotted with her so he'd moved away from home. Shunned Bayside, if he was being honest, which he hated being because then he had to admit that he'd been selfish.

He'd turned his back on his family, on his town and on the *Bugle*.

"How long are you going to beat yourself up for that?" Riley asked gently, kindly.

Sawyer shrugged. He'd put his parents through hell. Just another reason why the *Bugle* couldn't fail now. He would make sure of it.

Riley stepped closer. "You know, everyone has at least one bad relationship under their belt."

Something crossed her face. He wanted to jump on it and ask her what caused those shadows to appear, but she beat him to it.

"Heck, most people have multiple crappy relationships. You and Rachel lived in DC for a hot minute. And you came to your senses and moved back."

"I don't want to talk about Rachel."

"That's fine. What do you want to talk about?"

"How about you?"

She rolled her eyes.

"You look beautiful tonight."

He didn't know why he'd said that. It just slipped out. Her eyes widened in surprise. Had he never told her how gorgeous she was before? Riley was an insanely appealing woman who lit up any room she entered. Somehow she had the ability to be both the girl next door and the fantasy.

He didn't know when she'd reached that status. She'd been a cute kid. Freckles and pigtails and skinned knees. She'd been kind of an annoying preteen, always following him around at family functions. Maybe the change had occurred during high school, or college, when he was away too often to take note? Who the hell knew.

Right now, he couldn't take his eyes off her.

"Oh," she said to his comment. She scrunched up her nose, something he often saw her do at work.

Sawyer never danced at these events. Ever. So he was more shocked than anyone when he blurted out, "Dance with me."

Riley couldn't contain her surprise at the statement, either. Her green eyes widened. "Are you serious? You can't dance."

"I can." He reached for her hand. Her skin was so soft, so smooth. Like silk. "I just choose not to most of the time." He led her to the dance floor.

"What makes tonight the exception?" she asked, her voice husky.

You. But he couldn't say that. Shouldn't say that. This

was Riley, after all. Riley Hudson. Lifelong friend. Close family acquaintance. Employee. Gorgeous redhead who managed to sneak into his thoughts more than he'd like to admit.

"Tonight is a celebration," he said instead. He could tell she had another question, so he drew her to him, pressing one hand to her back and the other wrapped around her tiny, delicate hand.

And then all questions stopped. In fact, all talking ceased. While he was sure there was music playing, he didn't seem to hear it. Because being this close to Riley, inhaling her sweet perfume, taking in her tempting red lips, took over all his senses. It was like he didn't have room to notice anything else.

It should have been weird. Or awkward, at least. But for the first time, he wasn't thinking of her as his oldest friend or the kid he'd grown up with. She was an adult now and his body was taking notice.

He drew her closer. Her body felt good up against his. His hand traveled over the exposed skin of her back. He could feel her breath tickling his neck as she moved closer to him.

He had no idea how long they danced, Riley in his arms as they swayed to a song. Two songs? More than two songs?

Sawyer would have remained just like that forever but Jasper Dumont appeared at his side.

"Sorry to interrupt, guys."

Riley jumped back, a deer-in-headlights expression on her face. She gave Sawyer a long once-over before mumbling something and quickly making her way off the dance floor.

"Riley, wait," he called. Shoot. What had just happened? Seriously, what the hell had just freaking happened between them?

"Sorry, dude," Jasper said, a sheepish expression on his face. "I didn't mean to…" He gestured between Sawyer and Riley's retreating back.

"No, don't worry about it. We were just dancing."

Jasper's eyebrow quirked as the two of them made their way toward one of the bars. "Just dancing, huh? Trust me, I know all about *just* dancing. Well, I am sorry, but I interrupted for good reason. There's someone here who really wants to meet you." He turned to the man next to him. "This is—"

"Dan Melwood."

Sawyer accepted the handshake from the tall man with dark hair, just beginning to gray at the temples.

"Dan was born in New York but he lived in Bayside during his high school years," Jasper said. "He left years ago and is an entrepreneur who is considering adding to our local economy. Dan, this is—"

"Sawyer Wallace," Dan once again jumped in. "Publisher of the *Bayside Bugle*."

Sawyer raised a brow. "Publisher, editor in chief, reporter, head of ad sales, you name it. Life at a small-town newspaper."

Jasper left them to talk. Sawyer and Dan grabbed drinks at the bar and moved to a quiet corner. Dan was in his fifties, only a little younger than Sawyer's parents. As Jasper had informed him, Dan graduated from Bayside High, went off to college and business school, and then spent the next couple of decades building his businesses. He dabbled in real estate and construction. He explained to Sawyer that occasionally he invested in struggling companies, helping them improve their processes so they could turn a profit. Sounded like he'd helped out quite a few restaurants and commercial businesses in the state.

Now he was interested in Bayside. Particularly in the *Bugle*. He seemed to know a lot about newspapers, as if he'd done his research. Sawyer was impressed.

"I have to admit that I'm intrigued by this Bayside Blogger you have in the Style and Entertainment section."

Sawyer fought an urge that was somewhere between pride for Riley and protectiveness over her. "The Bayside Blogger is certainly our most popular column." He offered a small chuckle.

"And your most enigmatic."

Dan's smile faltered. Just slightly and only for a fraction of a second. But it was long enough for Sawyer to note.

"The blogger is definitely mysterious."

"And not always accurate."

Sawyer took a step back. "Actually, the one rule I've made with the blogger is that every article, every tidbit of gossip has to be true."

"That's interesting," Dan said, rubbing a hand along his jaw. "She happened to write about me last summer."

Sawyer racked his brain and then remembered. "Oh, yes," he said, choking slightly on bourbon. "I vaguely recall the piece. Maybe that's why your name is so familiar."

"I was back here visiting for a month or so. I can assure you what she wrote was not true."

He couldn't remember exactly what Riley had written, but he made a mental note to go back through the archives when he left tonight. Sawyer prided himself on journalistic integrity. It was the number-one thing he required of all his reporters. "I apologize if that's true.

I will certainly speak with the blogger and we'll print a correction if it turns out we were wrong."

Dan's face paled slightly. "Don't worry about that. Anyway, I won't leave you in suspense any longer. There's a reason I wanted to meet you tonight and talk about the paper."

Sawyer perked up and put his empty drink on a nearby table.

"I know it's hard times for print publications," Dan said.

Not what Sawyer had been expecting to hear. It was also a subject that he went out of his way to avoid. He had so much to figure out in the next couple of months. No matter what, he had to save his family's legacy.

Dan leaned closer. "Quite frankly, I can't believe you've lasted this long."

"A lot of new businesses have been flooding the area. That's helped," Sawyer explained. "Our online edition is going strong and we're utilizing our new app, and social media, of course."

"All good things. And I'd like to discuss this more in depth because I want to make a proposal."

Sawyer was all ears.

"I suggest that I come on board as a partner for the *Bugle*. I can offer you financial support, and maybe together we can figure out a way to save the newspaper."

Sawyer wanted to jump for joy, but he spotted his father across the dance floor. His head was tilted toward his mother's ear and, whatever he was saying, his mom was laughing hysterically.

Every single person in the Wallace family who had touched the *Bugle* had left an indelible mark on it. His father, in particular, had really done his best to keep the paper afloat. He'd been the one to go digital, long before most small-town newspapers looked to the internet.

Legacy firmly in mind, he refocused on Dan. "That's quite an offer. But, as I'm sure you know, the *Bugle* is a family-run business. It's been in the Wallace family since its launch issue."

"I realize that. In fact, I heard you're celebrating the one hundred and fiftieth anniversary this year. Quite a milestone. But, as I told you, I have made my fortune on turning around failing businesses."

"Do you have any experience in media?"

Dan's head bounced from side to side as he considered. "Some, but print media is a bit of a passion project for me." He swirled the amber liquid that was in his glass. "I already have some numbers put together for you. Why don't I revise them a bit? We can discuss investor options or even silent partnership."

Sawyer didn't know what to say. This was more than he could have asked for. "I'm overwhelmed," Sawyer admitted easily.

"There's only one thing I'd like in return."

At that moment, he heard Riley's laugh from the bar where she was talking to Jasper and Carissa. She threw her head back, exposing her long neck. She had the most beautiful laugh.

"What do you think?"

Embarrassed that he'd tuned out this possible *Bayside Bugle* savior, Sawyer struggled to refocus and get his mind off of Riley's…everything. "I'm sorry. I didn't quite catch that." He indicated the speakers, hoping Dan would think he hadn't heard over the noise.

Dan clapped a hand on his arm. "If I'm going to become involved in the *Bugle*, I want to be involved in every area."

Made sense to Sawyer. Who wouldn't want to know where their money was going?

"Meaning," Dan continued, "that I would want to know about every nook and cranny. Every secret. In particular, I will need to know the identity of the Bayside Blogger."

Sawyer froze just as Riley caught his gaze. She smiled at him.

Well, *damn*.

Chapter Three

Happy Tgiving! Hope all my gossip birdies are enjoying their family time. I know at least one person who will be eating her pumpkin pie alone. Poor little Riley Hudson has no one to watch the Macy's parade with since her parents swapped turkey day for a tropical cruise this year!

Sawyer scrolled through the Bayside Blogger's latest article. His finger hovered over the screen when he read the last part of the column.

He sighed. Riley didn't usually post things like that, especially about herself. After all, it wasn't as though she was alone. The Wallaces were hosting Thanksgiving this year and had invited her, along with half the town. Mr. and Mrs. Dumont would be there, as well as Cam, Elle, Jasper, Carissa, Elle's dad, Carissa's aunt and more. Riley was as much a part of his family as he was.

He reread the tweet one more time and considered shooting her a quick text of encouragement. But she'd been acting weird all week, avoiding eye contact with him and even working from home one day.

He could pretend to be oblivious, but he knew exactly why she was acting odd. That dance at Elle and Cam's engagement party. Something had shifted in their relationship and he would be outright lying if he didn't fess up to being shaken by it, as well.

He'd had no business dancing with her in that way. They'd been friends for far too long for one dance to feel like that.

Sawyer pulled his car up to his parents' house, put it in Park, but made no move to get out just yet.

Despite the three-day workweek, he'd been busy. He'd met with Dan Melwood and he was no closer to giving him a decision on his proposal than he had been at the party last Saturday. He'd asked for time to consider all options.

Dan was offering full financial assistance as the main investor. If Sawyer agreed, he wouldn't have to lay anyone off and he'd save his family's business. It also provided him with some wiggle room so he could play around with a couple ideas of branching out. Even with financial help now, at some point, he would be right back in the same position.

If he looked at the situation from that side, he'd be a fool not to accept what Dan was offering. But there was another side.

Riley.

Or the Bayside Blogger, he amended quickly. Dan wanted to know the identity of the Bayside Blogger. He claimed that as an investor, he was owed that right.

After Sawyer researched Riley's old columns, he'd figured out why the man was upset. Apparently, last summer, Dan had returned to Bayside for a month or so. Riley had insinuated that Dan had carried on an affair with a local woman. She hadn't named the woman. She hadn't even said the word "affair." But it was clearly implied what Dan had been up to.

Sawyer also learned that Dan and his wife separated after the summer. Coincidence? Probably not.

But what Dan was proposing was wrong, both morally and ethically. Sawyer wanted to save the paper, but was he ready to stoop to this level to get it done?

Sawyer pushed a hand through his hair. The only restriction Sawyer ever put on Riley in her position as the *Bugle*'s gossip columnist was that she be absolutely positive about the accuracy of anything she committed to print, and she'd never failed him. Not once. If she said Dan was carrying on an affair, he was.

He couldn't out her, though. She would be beyond humiliated. Sure, Dan was only one person. But he could easily share Riley's alter ego with another person. And that person could tell someone else. And so on. That was exactly why neither he nor Riley ever talked about the blogger. He hadn't even told his parents.

Speaking of his parents, maybe he should vet this whole situation with them. Since the newspaper didn't have a board, it would be nice to have someone to talk to about this. Although, that would mean revealing the financial trouble the paper was in. His dad would launch into a lecture about how he shouldn't be publishing every day of the week. A fact that Sawyer was proud of. He wanted to make his mark on the *Bugle*, too.

A rap on the car window scared the crap out of him. He turned to see his father standing next to the car with a questioning look on his face. Sawyer grabbed the bottle of wine and flowers he'd picked up for his mother and got out of the car.

"Everything okay, son?" his dad asked.

Henry Wallace had the same mischievous smile Sawyer was constantly told that he possessed. They were the same height and same build, with wide shoulders and long legs. They also shared a love of mystery books, seafood and fishing.

"I'm fine." He embraced his dad. "Happy Thanksgiving, Dad."

"Happy Thanksgiving. Come in." They walked down the path that, in the warmer months, was lined with flowers. Twin pots of mums flanked the door of the colonial two-story house that sat right off the bay.

"How's the *Bugle*?"

"Everything's great." It was a standard answer he gave his dad, but he felt guilty, nonetheless. At some point, he needed to tell his father the true picture of what was happening. But once he did that, everything would be more real.

Henry made to open the door, then suddenly covered the handle with his hand and gave his son a long once-over. "You know, you can always talk to me. About anything."

Sawyer felt like he was back in high school being questioned about making out with his girlfriend or drinking after the big game. "I know."

"Because I do have some experience in the newspaper biz."

He certainly did. Sawyer had always looked up to his father. Idolized him, really. And not only because of his role at the *Bugle*. People in the community respected him, valued his opinion. He was a family man. Loyal to the very end.

Everything Sawyer wished he could be.

"I've heard that somewhere," Sawyer said as they finally entered the house. Immediately, they were assaulted with the aromas of Thanksgiving. The smell of sage and roasting turkey wafted out to greet him, as did all of the spices of pumpkin pie, yams and his mother's famous green bean casserole.

"But what I want to talk about is your retirement. Heard your golf game is actually regressing."

Henry stopped walking and wagged a finger in his face. "You've been talking to your mother. Never listen to her."

"I heard that," Patty Wallace called from the kitchen.

Sawyer and his dad exchanged a look before entering the room. As soon as they did, a flurry of activity greeted them in the way of hugs, handshakes and holiday greetings. Someone thrust a mug of spiked cider into his hand and his mother was fussing over him and thanking him for the flowers.

But Sawyer was busy surveying the room. A lot of their guests had already arrived, but not everyone.

"Where's Riley?" he asked his mom.

His mother patted his cheek. "She should be here soon. She was making that whipped Jell-O you like this morning."

"But she's coming, right?"

His mother cocked her head curiously. "Of course. Why would you ask that? She's spent practically every Thanksgiving here since she was in diapers."

"I know, it's just…" He trailed off because he didn't really want to get into her tweet with his mom.

"If I know Riley, she'll be flouncing through the door at any minute in a fabulous outfit."

"Did someone say my name?"

Sawyer twisted his head so fast he almost got whiplash. Just as his mother had suggested, there she stood in a forest-green sweater and polka-dot pants. She'd left her hair down in loose curls and it was bouncing around her as she entered the room carrying a covered dish and a bottle of wine.

Riley was greeted even more enthusiastically than he'd been. He moved to welcome her but was blocked by the entrance of Elle and Cam.

Elle, Carissa and Riley were in the midst of planning Elle's bridal shower, so it didn't surprise Sawyer to see the three of them joined at the hip all afternoon. They helped his mother in the kitchen, enjoyed wine in the family room while football blared from the television.

Every time Sawyer made a move to get closer to her, someone would intervene. Or a timer would go off in the kitchen and Riley would race away. Or one of her friends would want to show her something on their phone. Or she'd refill her drink.

The universe was clearly against him.

He thought dinner would help. He and Riley usually sat at the far end of the long dining room table. But this year, there had been a seating adjustment. Instead of sitting next to his oldest friend, he strained to hear her hearty laugh from way at the other end of the room. He couldn't even enjoy his mother's turkey, which was always amazing.

The real question was whether Riley was actually avoiding him or if all of the distractions were coincidental. He got that their dance the other night had been a little much. Hell, he was still thinking about it. All the time. But that was no reason to avoid someone you've known your whole life.

In any case, he resolved during dessert and more football that he would get to the bottom of her cold shoulder. Just then, opportunity presented itself when Riley went out on the deck. Alone. Sawyer jumped up, grabbed a fresh beer and joined her.

It was cold and the breeze coming off the bay didn't help matters. His parents had started a fire in the family room and the smell of wood smoke was a comforting and autumnal aroma.

Riley had wrapped one of his mother's throw blankets around herself. She was standing at the far end of the deck, away from the windows of the family room. Her glass of wine sat on the banister, untouched. She was lost in her thoughts, staring out at the water.

He quietly approached, suddenly unsure what to say. The moonlight played over her face and he longed to reach out and touch her.

"Hey, Ri," he finally said.

Riley jumped a mile and then spun around. Her wine glass wobbled but luckily didn't take the plunge over the railing.

She placed a hand over her chest. "Good grief, Sawyer. Where'd you come from?"

"That's a very esoteric question. How deep do you want to get tonight?"

She smiled at him and he felt it all the way in his gut.

"I never get deep unless I've had at least three pieces of pumpkin pie. Right now, I'm only up to two."

He joined her at the railing and put down his beer bottle. "Are you warm enough?"

She nodded. "I'm fine. I needed some air."

The two of them had never had any problem keeping a conversation going, yet tonight it felt strained. Awkward.

"Listen, Ri," he said.

"Hey, Sawyer," Riley said at the same time.

They laughed. "Go ahead," she said.

He wanted to ask about their dance. Wanted to know if it had made her feel the same way he'd felt that night. Wanted to know if her feelings about him were starting to change too. Instead, he said, "I saw your column this morning. I didn't realize you were upset about your parents' cruise. Why didn't you tell me?"

She shrugged and continued to look out over the water. "You know how it is. Sometimes we don't realize how we feel about something until we write it down."

True. Which was exactly why he needed to stay clear of any kind of writing assignment at the moment. His emotions and feelings were too jumbled. Making sense of them might just scare him.

Riley took a sip of her wine. "I don't know why I'm even bothered about my parents. They deserve this vacation and they'll be back next week. I guess… I mean… it's only that I miss them and…"

He reached for her arm and turned her to face him. "What, Riley?"

"I'm lonely."

It was such an un-Riley-like statement and the combination of her words and the frightened expression on her face was like a punch to his gut.

"Oh, hon, why? They're only on vacation for ten days. You just said so yourself."

Her eyes were looking everywhere but at his. "It's not just that. It's stupid, really."

"We've been friends for a million years. You can tell me anything."

She finally met his gaze. "Friends. Right." She tightened the blanket around her. "Elle is engaged and Carissa is going to be moving in with Jasper. Plus, she's also…"

He cocked his head. "She's what?"

Riley shook her head. "Never mind. It's nothing. The point is that Elle and Carissa are both making huge changes."

So that's what this mood was about. Her two closest

friends were taking big steps in their lives and relationships.

"And you wish you were in a relationship, too?" he asked. He held his breath, uncertain of what he wanted to hear her say.

"Yes. No." She shook her head. "I don't know. It's not that."

He leaned toward her. "What is it?"

"It's confusing and…and…"

"Ri," he said, his voice sounding husky even to his ears.

"Sawyer, I don't know…" She gestured helplessly between them.

He reached for her hand. It was so small wrapped up in his. When he met her gaze again, he saw something he'd never seen there before. At least, not whenever she'd looked at him. But there it was, pure lust. And he knew exactly how she felt.

Without analyzing it, he did what felt natural to him. He pulled her to him and covered her lips with his.

For the second time that night, Sawyer shocked her. But this time, he wasn't sneaking up on her. He was kissing her.

And quite well.

His lips moved over hers, softly at first. Her surprise lasted for only a second and, before she knew it, her hands were winding up around his neck, the blanket she'd wrapped herself in falling to the floor of the deck.

He pulled her even closer as his lips became more and more greedy. His hands were in her hair and then moved down her body until they reached her hips.

He smelled so good. His cologne was tickling her nose as she ripped her lips away to place a soft kiss against the column of his neck, apparently a sensitive spot. He made a sound, something like a growl, and feasted on her lips once more.

Riley felt like stars were exploding around her. She hadn't experienced pure, unadulterated passion like this since...

Suddenly she pushed away from him. They were both struggling for breath, their chests mirroring each other in a rapid up-and-down rhythm.

"I can't," she said in a very unsteady voice.

"I'm sorry," he said, his eyes wide and dark with desire.

She wasn't sorry. Not in the least. That was part of the problem. She couldn't kiss Sawyer. He was her friend, not to mention that he currently handed out her paycheck.

But it had felt so good, so natural.

No. She shook her head, trying desperately to clear it. At the same time, she shivered.

"Ri," Sawyer said, bending to retrieve the blanket. "You're going to get sick. Here." He placed the blanket around her shoulders, adjusting it so that it covered all of her. He lingered, and his fingers brushed over her collarbone, inciting another shiver that had nothing to do with the weather.

Sawyer must have noticed and his eyes focused on her lips. Before she could protest, he was tugging the blanket toward him, which had the added effect of bringing her right to him. She raised her head. Big mistake—it put his sumptuous mouth in front of her.

How could she resist?

They stood like that for a moment. A long, heated moment. She didn't know who moved first. Maybe it was both of them. She let out a gasp, and then once again their lips met.

Who knew Sawyer Wallace could kiss like this? If he wasn't holding her up by the blanket, her knees would give out.

After what felt like hours, they parted. Gently he kissed the tip of her nose and then her forehead before pulling her in for a long hug.

"Riley, that was—"

"Something that absolutely cannot happen again," she finished sadly.

He released her and pinned her with questioning eyes. "Ri," he began. Instead of finishing, he scratched his head. "Are you seeing someone?"

"No, of course not. You'd know if I were."

"Then what?"

"It's not you, Sawyer. It's me. I can't do *that* with you."

After their dance at Elle and Cam's engagement party last week, this kiss wasn't really a surprise. When they'd danced, it had felt like they were the only two people in Bayside. And that had scared the crap out of her.

She'd spent the week avoiding him, which frankly hadn't been that hard. He'd met with Dan Melwood. Riley wondered what that was about. Dan had been in Bayside last summer, but as far as she knew he didn't have any reason to be back so soon.

"Talk to me," he said firmly.

She put space between them. Bided her time by taking a sip of her wine. She owed him some kind of explanation.

"Okay." She nodded. "When I lived in New York, there was a guy there. A guy that I dated."

"I always wondered," he said more to himself.

"We worked together."

"Ah." He ran a hand through his hair. "Let me guess. There was a policy against dating in your office?"

"Actually, no." She drank a much bigger sip of wine. "I wish there would have been. But I was young and stupid so I probably would have ignored it anyway." She tightened the blanket around her. "Connor and I hit it off right away. Before I knew it, we were dating."

Sawyer's face was serious. "What happened with him?"

"He got promoted." She swallowed hard. "To my supervisor."

"Damn."

"Exactly," Riley agreed. "I don't need to go into all the details."

More like, she didn't want to go into the details, because if she did, Sawyer would know that she was a major idiot. She'd have to tell him how wonderful she'd thought Connor was. How she'd stupidly thought they would get engaged and married one day. How she made him the center of her universe only to have that universe come crashing down around her when she learned that Connor was already engaged to another woman.

There had been signs, but she'd ignored them. Connor had made a fool out of her and out of her belief in love.

"Riley," Sawyer urged.

She opened her eyes. She hadn't even realized she'd closed them. "He became my boss and the situation became so complicated."

"He didn't fire you, did he?"

Was it her imagination or was a vein ticking in his neck? It was too dark to tell.

"No, he didn't fire me. It was an incredibly uncomfortable couple of months. I tried to find work elsewhere, but nothing panned out."

"So you came back home to Bayside," Sawyer said.

"Not at first. I wanted to give it some time, see if

things got better. But after four years in New York I was ready to return."

"I see."

"Do you?" she asked. "When I came home, I promised myself that I would never, ever put myself in a situation like that again."

"A situation where you date your boss."

"A situation where I could possibly humiliate myself. That's why I can't kiss you. Or date you. Not now, not ever. Even if I want to."

He stepped closer. "Do you? Do you want to kiss me?"

She held up a hand. "It doesn't matter what I want, Sawyer. The fact is, nothing can happen between us. You're my boss."

"I'm your friend, too, and I always will be."

Yes, he was. Another stark reminder. Kissing him had the potential to damage both their working relationship and friendship. Not to mention the drama that would ensue if anyone found out about them. And Riley just couldn't—*wouldn't*—go through that again.

Chapter Four

Ho-ho-ho, Baysiders! Who else is excited for today's Christmas Kickoff Festival? You know I'll be mingling in the crowd. Hopefully, Santa won't put me on the naughty list. But I'll tell you someone who should be...;)

Sawyer's plan for the town's annual Christmas Kickoff Festival was to do a quick lap to check out the scene, stop at The Brewside for coffee and then get back to the action.

He'd attended this festival every year of his life except for two. He shook his head, willing the guilt over that lapse in judgment to fade.

Instead, he took in the center of the town square where a huge Christmas tree had been erected, decorated and awaited the ceremony tonight, when its hundreds of strands of lights would illuminate the square. A cute picket fence surrounded the tree, and an old-fashioned electric train made its way around the base. Sawyer had loved trains when he was a boy and just seeing the one today brought back all kinds of warm childhood memories.

Beyond the train were oversize presents wrapped in red, green, gold and silver paper. He was happy to see the large bins on the other side of the tree that had been set up to collect toys and coats for local charities, too. He needed to remember to bring the things he'd bought for that. Maybe they could even take up a collection at the *Bugle*.

More guilt washed over him. How could he ask his employees for donations to charity when he might have to lay some of them off soon?

Sawyer wished he could go one day without thinking about all of the troubles in his life. Especially at this time of year. He cared about each and every person on his staff, almost as if they were family. Until he knew they were taken care of, he'd never stop worrying.

Once again, he pushed his thoughts to the back of his mind and continued his lap of the square. Every business boasted wreaths, garlands and decorations in their windows. From experience, he knew they would all be outlined in twinkly lights, as well. Lampposts, benches and pretty much all free space in the town square had been devoted to the holiday cause.

He had to admit the festival was always fun, but this year the town council had gone all-out. A band was on a stage playing lively carols. Some of the businesses displayed tables and stands outside of their doors with special festival prices. Stands were set up throughout the square selling holiday cookies and other baked goods. Sawyer knew Carissa had provided some of them. She'd left Thanksgiving early last night to bake. They also had coffee, tea, cider and hot chocolate.

Sawyer hoped that with all the beverages outside there wouldn't be a line in The Brewside, but as he pushed through the door, he saw he was out of luck. As the town's favorite source of caffeine and a great gossip hotspot, the place was always busy.

Situated between a shoe store and a high-end clothing shop, the coffeehouse had the same look of the other shops around the square. They were all painted white with blue shutters. He noticed quite a few pots of poinsettias beside the entrances.

In Sawyer's opinion, each store on the square was unique, but The Brewside was the only one that felt like home. It was cozy with its quaint decor, raised ceiling made up of exposed beams and dark wood floors. Tony had decorated it with antiques like old vinyl records, framed black-and-white photos and old-fashioned kitchen items. His favorite piece was the refurbished brass cash register that sat on the long bar.

The staff had already put up their Christmas tree in one corner. Sawyer knew that Tony encouraged the local elementary school kids to donate homemade ornaments. Stockings with the employees' names hung behind the counter, and poinsettias dominated every free space.

He offered a wave and a nod to Tony, owner of the joint, and got in line. As he waited his turn, he tuned into a conversation between two women about the Bayside Blogger.

"I mean, she didn't really write anything scandalous today," one of them said.

"Well, yesterday *was* Thanksgiving. Maybe she's in a food coma like the rest of us. Or maybe she went to the amazing Black Friday sales at the outlets at four in the morning like we did," the other woman contributed.

"Or maybe she doesn't have any gossip today."

The two women looked at each other for a beat. Simultaneously they shook their heads and laughed. "Nah," they said together.

Sawyer pushed a hand through his hair. The women were right. Riley not having gossip was like The Brewside not having any customers. Unlikely.

Besides, he knew firsthand that she happened to have one hell of a scoop. He could just see her column now.

Everyone's favorite editor was spotted making out in the dark shadows of his parents' deck last night. Guess someone's lips tasted better than the pumpkin pie!

Riley *had* tasted better than pumpkin pie. Better than every other dessert combined.

When he let himself think about their kiss—*really* think about it—the air left his body. He'd kissed his fair share of women over the years, and none had felt like that.

He kept mulling over their conversation just before the kiss, when she'd admitted she was lonely. Confessed that it was a little difficult to watch her two best friends find such happy relationships. Did Riley *want* to date someone? Did she want to be in a relationship?

Did he want to date her?

The thought surprised him so much that he actually took a step backward. Whoa. Where had that come from?

He certainly wanted to kiss her more.

She was his friend, who could kiss like a dream and who, if he was being truly honest, had started becoming more to him over the last couple of years.

She was also his employee. He was her boss, as she'd pointed out last night. He'd been glad she'd opened up about her time in New York City, although he did suspect there was more to that story. Still, she'd told him she would never date her boss again. Never put herself in that position again.

So, he needed to stop thinking about her in that way. Even if he would give up The Brewside's coffee for the rest of his life for one more chance at feeling her lips against his. One more time to...

"Yo! Sawyer, dude."

His head snapped up at the sound of Tony's amused voice. Heat rushed into his face. "Sorry."

Tony gestured to him. "Sawyer Wallace, everyone. Our esteemed editor in chief."

Sawyer received a nice little round of applause. He bowed and then stepped up to Tony to place his order.

"Sorry, man," he repeated.

"No worries." Tony accepted Sawyer's frequent-customer card and cash. "I mean, I saw you standing there. I know you were physically in the room. But mentally?" He whistled. "You were on a planet in a galaxy far, far away." He punched the card and gave it back. "Working on a big story?"

"Nah. Just this holiday festival. Lots to cover."

"Yeah, Riley was in here earlier complaining..." He trailed off, catching himself. "Did I say complaining? I meant, she was excitedly chatting about how much she loves her job."

Sawyer accepted his extra-large black coffee and chuckled. "I just bet."

"Oh, I almost forgot. Some guy named Dan Melwood was in here asking about you. Actually, about you and the Bayside Blogger."

That got Sawyer's full attention. "Really?"

Tony nodded. "Who is he? Gotta admit, I didn't get a great feeling from him."

Despite being everyone's favorite resident now, Tony wasn't a Bayside native. He'd met his wife, a local woman named Georgia Cooper, in college, and they'd started The Brewside when they'd moved back to town after getting married. Sawyer didn't know all the details but, unfortunately, he did know that the marriage hadn't lasted. Georgia had hightailed it out of Bayside and Tony had stayed. The town had come to love him as their own.

Sawyer explained who Dan Melwood was. "What did he ask about the blogger?"

"The usual questions. Do I know who it is, that kind of thing." Tony paused, considering. "But he seemed *really* intent on finding out her identity. I mean, who isn't?" Tony's face fell.

"What is it?" Sawyer asked.

"He wouldn't let it go. Made me feel a little protective of her. Or him, although most people do think it's a her. But whoever the blogger is, I found myself defending her." Tony held up a finger. "Even though she did write last week that I hadn't been on a date in three years and wouldn't know what to do if I were to go out with someone."

Sawyer cringed. *Dammit, Ri.* "Sorry about that."

Tony offered a good-natured smile. "Not the worst thing she's ever written. Besides, she brings people into this place. She writes about The Brewside so often that people think she's going to be here. So in they come."

"Everyone in town is always here."

Tony nodded emphatically. "Exactly."

Sawyer raised his cup of coffee in salute. "Happy to help. And let me know if Dan asks you any more questions."

"Will do," Tony agreed as Sawyer exited The Brewside.

He didn't like the idea of Dan badgering Tony or anyone else in town. He knew that what Riley had written about him had been intense—tougher than she usually went on people. Still, everything had been true.

To hear that Dan was asking questions at The Brewside made him seem obsessed at this point.

Journalism ran in Sawyer's blood. Part of that was a distinct nudging, a reporter's hunch. In any case, he was feeling it now. What exactly did Dan plan to do with the knowledge of the blogger's identity if and when he got it?

If Dan only wanted to know for himself, that was one thing. Maybe Sawyer could live with that. But if he wanted to take it further and reveal Riley's secret to the entire town... There was no way Sawyer could let that happen.

The only thing that was keeping him from telling Dan Melwood to take a hike was the chance that his investment in the paper could save jobs for the rest of the staff.

The other big question regarding Riley was what Sawyer was going to do about that kiss.

Sawyer continued walking toward the festival, stopping frequently to chat as he ran into family and friends. He checked in with his reporters as he saw them interviewing people, taking photos and jotting notes for their stories.

The ceremony portion of the festival started. The mayor gave a speech as the town council and Santa Claus joined him onstage. Sawyer made to move closer to the stage until he spotted Dan Melwood in the crowd. He really didn't feel like dealing with the man at the moment, so Sawyer averted his eyes and quickly made his way into the shadows. He saw an isolated spot between two of the buildings that actually had a great view of the stage and Christmas tree. He took another step and ran right into— "Riley?"

"Ow! Hey—oh, Sawyer?"

"What are you doing hiding here?"

She poked him in the chest with her index finger. "I could ask you the same thing. Are you following me?"

He took her in. She was wearing tight dark jeans, tall gray boots and a matching gray wool peacoat, which was pretty subdued for her. But she'd accentuated it with a large sparkly pin, purple leather gloves and one of those fleece headbands that covered her ears and had a large purple flower right on the front. Her cheeks were pink from the cold weather and her lips… Her pink lips were adorably pouted as she questioned him.

"I'm not following you. But I think we had the same idea."

She shook her head, curls bouncing around that headband. "Nope. I don't think so. I picked out this spot days ago to watch the tree lighting because it's a great vantage point. You, my friend," she said with another poke to his chest, "are hiding. The question remains, who are you hiding from?"

"I don't know. Are you asking me or is this an inquisition by the Bayside Blogger?"

She gave him a "duh" look. "Uh, the blogger. I'm here on your dime today."

He leaned against the wall to give himself some space. Standing that close to her had her rose-smelling perfume infiltrating his senses and shutting down his brain. "Sorry about that. How's the coverage going?"

She took a moment, considering with a cute little head tilt. "Okay. We definitely got more than in years past."

"But?" he guessed.

"But if the town council had given us more time, more of a heads-up that they were trying to turn our little small-town Christmas festival into something grandiose, I could have done even more. Maybe a cool online piece."

She was always so hard on herself. The Bayside Blogger aside, Riley was one of his best reporters. She was a fast writer who needed little editing, and she had an intuitive knack for interviewing people and getting them to reveal the real story. Not to mention she was an ace when it came to social media. "I'm sure what you got will be amazing. I liked the pre-event coverage."

She rapped him on the chest for the third time. "Again,

it would have been better if I'd been given more time. We could have done a contest for the kids. Or we could have created some Facebook and Instagram ads. With a little more money toward—"

"We don't have the money for…" Realizing his mistake, he let the sentence trail off and prayed that Riley wouldn't pick up on it. Naturally, she did.

"Sawyer?"

"Don't start," he said, throwing his hand up for emphasis.

"I'm not. It's just that—"

"It's nothing," he said. But the statement didn't seem to appease her any more than it calmed him.

The *Bugle was* in trouble, a fact that he wanted to keep to himself for as long as possible. At least, until he had a viable solution.

His earlier thought of Riley's great journalistic skills was backfiring on him. She had that look in her eyes, that glimmer of a story.

"But you said we don't have money. I've asked you this before and I'm going to ask you again. Is the *Bugle* in trouble?"

Those keen green eyes narrowed as she searched his face for any kind of tell. It wasn't that he didn't trust Riley, but admitting the failings of the newspaper out loud would make it real. And Sawyer desperately wished that none of this were real.

"How about this? When I need to talk to you about the newspaper, I will." She didn't seem placated. "You will be the *first* person I talk to."

"Do I have a choice in the matter?"

"Not really." He shifted his weight and changed the subject. "Heard some people talking about you in The Brewside."

One of her eyebrows rose in a delicate arch. "Me or my alter ego?"

"Your alter ego, of course. They were surprised you didn't have any good gossip today."

She rolled her eyes. "Oh, please. Ye of little faith. I've been tweeting up a storm since I got here. Sharon Wright and Elliot Walker were totally getting it on behind the Boathouse."

"No kidding?"

She grinned. "This is an interesting development because Elliot only got out of a serious relationship like a month ago. He'd been dating Amanda Wright for four years and Amanda told everyone with ears that she dumped him because he had no sense of spontaneity or passion." She snorted. "He certainly looked, ah, passionate to me."

She was on a roll now and Sawyer enjoyed watching her eyes light up with enjoyment. "I also happened to notice Mrs. Glamore, the librarian at the public library, winking at Ted Owens."

Sawyer practically choked. "Elle's dad?"

"Hey, he's available."

"He's in his sixties," Sawyer countered.

"So what? Love has no age limits," Riley said passionately.

"Speaking of love, the women I overheard talking about you were also wondering if the Bayside Blogger had a boyfriend."

"Shut up."

She made to jab him and he easily caught her fist. His eyes searched hers before skimming down to take in that appealing heart-shaped mouth again.

"What are you doing?"

Her words snapped him out of it. "Uh, nothing."

"Well, stop it."

"Stop what?"

"Stop looking at me like you want to…like we've already…like you want to again…"

He couldn't stop himself. He cupped her cheek. "Maybe I do want to again."

"Well, you can't. We can't," she said even as she leaned into his palm.

Sawyer moved closer, his eyes intent on her lips. Riley shivered. Her eyes began to drift closed, and his followed as he imagined the softness of her mouth beneath his. Then a dazzling light had them flying open again. The Christmas tree had just been lit, and all of the shops and buildings lining the square—even some of the boats bobbing in the bay—were decorated in beautiful lights.

"Wow, beautiful," Riley whispered.

"Yes, you are."

He waited for her to hit him again or to at least roll her eyes. She didn't. Instead, she stood there, with those big green eyes, her face aglow from all of the twinkly lights.

He'd never wanted anyone more.

And she was the only woman he couldn't have. Ever.

Chapter Five

Well, well, well, looks like everyone's favorite high school
sweethearts, Jasper Dumont and Carissa Blackwell, are
moving in together. I heard that...
DELETE, DELETE, DELETE

Riley blew out a long, frustrated breath. She was having a major case of writer's block. No, not writer's block.
Blogger's block.

She stared at her computer screen, willing it to come
up with words on its own. When that didn't happen, she
tried again.

The usual suspects were all at the Wallace family house
for Thanksgiving last week. Including Bayside Bugle heir
and playboy Sawyer, who was looking fine. Especially
when he kissed his lifelong friend, Riley Hudson!

DELETE, DELETE, DELETE

She kept hitting the delete button long after all the
words were erased. And then she hit it one more time
for good measure.

Never in her entire career as the Bayside Blogger had
she struggled this much with her column. Maybe that
was because she'd never been part of the story before.

"You are a hypocrite, Riley Alexandra Hudson," she said to her empty apartment. Anyone else and she would have blogged about their first kiss so fast that it would have been posted before they came up for air.

However, most couples were probably happy about kissing, while she remained completely undecided.

It wasn't that she hadn't enjoyed it. She had. A lot. A whole heck of a lot. That was the problem. Besides being a beyond-stellar kisser, Sawyer happened to hold two other titles in her life: friend and boss.

Riley let out a long, deep groan and began circling her apartment. She loved this space. When Dumont Incorporated had erected this apartment building right in the center of town she'd jumped on it. Now she was the proud renter of an adorable one-bedroom with hardwood floors, tons of natural light, and killer views of the bay and the town square. Her kitchen was full of upgrades, her bathroom had an amazing soaking tub, and there were plenty of built-in shelves for all of her books and knick-knacks. And the closet had lots of room for her shoes. Many, many pairs of shoes.

Plus, it was decorated flawlessly, if she did say so herself. She'd opted for crisp white furniture and accented every room with pillows, artwork and accessories in every color of the rainbow.

She flopped onto her oversize couch—highlighted with turquoise, red and yellow throw pillows—and tapped a finger to her lips. Taking a deep breath, she inhaled the scent of the coffee she'd made earlier that morning, still lingering in the air.

She'd been down this road before. The "I kissed my boss" route to hell, and it had ended badly. She wrapped her arms around her stomach. Even after all these years, the pain was still fresh and she still felt raw. Connor had betrayed her trust. Not only had he been engaged to someone else while they dated, but once everything was out in the open, he'd let her take the blame for everything. Not once had he stepped in to clear her name.

If she closed her eyes, she could still see the judgy eyes of everyone she'd worked with. Every time she'd entered a room, the hair on the back of her neck had stood straight up, a sure sign everyone had been talking about her.

A loud banging on the door thankfully pulled her out of her head. She bounced to the door and greeted her two best friends.

"Who's ready for some serious downward dog?" Carissa asked, moving past Riley into the room.

"I would never miss our Saturday yoga dates," Riley said loyally.

The three of them headed to the yoga studio, only a block from Riley's apartment building. On the way, they chatted about the Christmas Kickoff Festival. While Elle and Carissa discussed the decorations, Riley couldn't help remembering the look in Sawyer's eyes as he'd cupped her face as he'd brought her closer to him.

"Hello," Elle's voice rang out. "Earth to Riley."

Riley shook her head. "Sorry, what?"

"I said, you'd better be on your best behavior."

Riley waved a nonchalant hand in the air as they strolled into the studio and stashed their stuff. "I don't know why the instructor is so hard on me."

Carissa unrolled her mat as the class assembled around them. "Kyra is hard on you because you never stop talking."

"Hey, that's not true."

Elle waited a beat before snorting. "Yoga is supposed to be calming and peaceful."

"Totally," Riley agreed, getting her own mat ready. "I'm always at peace in this class."

"You're the only one," Carissa said.

Undeterred, Riley stuck her tongue out at her.

Kyra, their instructor, entered the room then and glanced around the studio. "Good morning, everyone." She put on her favorite playlist and moved to her spot at the front of the room.

"Namaste," Riley offered heartily.

Carissa and Elle started laughing. Kyra gave a pained smile, then turned back to the class. "Time to forget the outside world, everyone. Center yourselves in the room. Focus on your breaths. In…and out." She moved into child's pose, and for the next hour, Riley did her best to concentrate on her breathing and how her body was feeling.

How what she'd like to be feeling was Sawyer's lips on hers again.

No, no, no. What is wrong with me! She let out a frustrated sound while everyone else exhaled the troubles from the week.

"What's wrong?" Elle whispered.

"Nothing," Riley said. "Do you want to grab coffee and some of those yummy glazed doughnuts after this?"

"Let us move our minds from the material world and take them to a place of reflection," Kyra's lyrical voice instructed. "A place where there are no glazed doughnuts."

"I'd like to go to a place where the glazed doughnuts didn't have any calories," Carissa said quietly. "I'm in for coffee and carbs."

"Me, too," Elle agreed. "I could use some non-wedding-planning girl time. I think Cam is hanging out with Sawyer today."

Riley stumbled. Her warrior pose was less warrior,

more cowardly lion. "Why are you asking me about Sawyer?" Riley asked defensively.

"I'm not," Elle said with a head tilt. "I just mentioned him in passing. Why are you getting so defensive?"

"And channel your inner child. Your inner *quiet* child. Your child that stops talking," Kyra said from the front of the room.

"Just because I've known him forever doesn't mean anything," Riley said. "And even though... Okay, okay, we may have kinda, sorta kissed."

Carissa and Elle both froze in the middle of their sun salutations.

"What!" Carissa blurted out loudly.

A resounding *shh* came from about six different people. Kyra tapped her foot in a very impatient way.

"Sorry," Carissa mumbled, and Elle snickered. "What?" she repeated in a much softer tone.

"I know. It's...shocking."

Her friends exchanged an amused look. "Um, yeah. You and Sawyer kissing is about as shocking as the sun rising in the east," Carissa said.

"What do you mean?"

Elle moved into child's pose but turned her head toward Riley. "After seeing the two of you dance at my engagement party, it was clear to the entire town just how much you guys are into each other."

"What are you talking about? We danced for one song."

Carissa snorted. "Try three songs in a row."

"Ladies," the yoga instructor said. "I'm going to have to ask you to lower your voices. Or, better yet, stop talking altogether. The quiet will help your mind and body connect."

"You're right. I'm sorry, Kyra," Riley said to the instructor.

Had she and Sawyer really danced for that long? Holy cow.

Somehow, and she truly had no idea how, Riley managed to finish class. At the same time, she was somewhat horrified she'd told Elle and Carissa about that kiss. Even though they were her very best friends, she just hadn't planned on opening up about something she couldn't quite understand herself yet.

Luckily, neither of them mentioned it again during class. And not on the walk to The Brewside, either. They ordered three coffees and a bunch of glazed doughnuts and found a somewhat private table in the back corner.

Maybe luck would be on her side and no one would mention Sawyer and kissing again.

"So? Are you ever going to tell us the details about this kiss or what?" Carissa asked, licking the glaze off her doughnut.

Riley sighed. Luck had never been her thing anyway. "I mean, there's not really much to tell."

"Um, there's a whole bunch to tell, so hop to it. Where? When? How long?" Elle was practically bouncing in her seat.

"Tongue?" Carissa added.

Riley rolled her eyes dramatically. "Were we at a seventh-grade dance? Of course there was tongue."

Elle pointed her doughnut at Riley. "See, I knew she would spill for carbs."

Carissa edged closer to Elle so they were shoulder to shoulder, a united front, staring her down. "You might as well tell us everything. We're not going to leave you alone until you do."

Riley held her ground. For all of point-three seconds.

Then she relented, took a huge bite of her doughnut with sprinkles and launched into the story.

"It was Thanksgiving night," she began.

"Hold up." Carissa pushed a finger into the air for emphasis. "We were there?"

"Yep."

Elle looked thoughtful. "Oh right. The two of you were out on the deck for a while after dinner."

"Right. We were just talking and I let it slip that I had been feeling kind of lonely."

Both sets of eyes watching her grew in size and filled with worry.

"Lonely?" Elle asked.

"Ri, what's wrong?" Carissa asked.

Riley waved her hand nonchalantly. "It's nothing. Just a passing feeling. I was missing my parents." As much as she loved her friends, she didn't want to tell them the full truth, which was that she'd been feeling left out since they'd both gotten into extremely serious relationships. She would never want them to feel bad. Besides, she was beyond happy for them.

Elle tilted her head, studying Riley. "Are you sure that's all it was?"

"Positive." Riley crossed her fingers under the table. "Anyway, Sawyer and I were talking about that and then one thing led to another... Next thing I know, we're kissing."

Neither Elle nor Carissa said anything for a moment. Finally Carissa beamed. "About freaking time."

"Totally," Elle agreed.

"What are you talking about?" Riley asked. Clearly her friends had lost their minds.

"You and Sawyer have this insane chemistry," Elle

said. "I noticed it as soon as I returned from Italy last year. It's palpable."

"What?" Riley felt completely gobsmacked. "We don't… I mean, we can't. It's too complicated."

"Because he's your boss?" Elle guessed, sympathy in her light green eyes.

"Yes. No." She shook her head. "Not exactly. I mean, he's my boss, but he's also my friend. My longtime family friend. And he knows…" She trailed off.

"He knows what?" Carissa asked. "Like some deep dark secret that you've been keeping from us?"

Riley gulped down her coffee. Hard. The liquid burned her throat. She coughed and turned her head, her gaze landing on a discarded copy of the *Bugle*, her latest Bayside Blogger post staring back at her. It felt like a huge neon light was pointing straight at her.

"Oh, please. Riley never hides stuff from us," Elle said loyally.

Maybe not, but right now she wanted to hide under the table.

"But going back to the amazing chemistry between you and Sawyer," Elle continued. "I even asked Car if you two had dated in the past, or were currently dating. Or, at the very least, hooking up."

"I knew you hadn't," Carissa piped in. "But I'm not sure why. The way he looks at you when he thinks you're not paying attention…" She whistled, long and low, and then fanned her face.

This was all news to Riley. She wanted to hear more about how Sawyer looked at her, but, instead, she focused on something else she'd noted. "Wait a minute. You guys have been talking about me and Sawyer?"

Elle nodded. "For months."

"You're lucky that we're the only ones talking about it," Carissa said.

"What do you mean?"

Carissa deliberated between two doughnuts before choosing a chocolate glazed. "I mean, you're lucky the Bayside Blogger hasn't mentioned you and Sawyer getting all smoochie-smoochie."

Oh, crap. "Uh, yeah, that is lucky." She swallowed. Hard. "But you know, how would she even know? Sawyer and I were out on his parents' deck. In the dark."

"How does she know anything? Come on. Think about all the embarrassing things she posted about me and Cam. And you and Jasper," Elle said to Carissa.

"She's such a beyotch," Carissa said.

"That's kind of strong," Riley said, trying to keep the defensiveness out of her voice.

"Oh, come on, Ri. She put me through hell."

"Yeah, but maybe she was just trying to help."

Carissa rolled her eyes. "Oh, please. Jasper and I almost didn't get together because of her meddling."

The comment was completely unexpected to Riley. And the complete opposite of what she'd thought. She liked to think that her blogs and tweets helped couples find each other. Like she was the final push they needed to realize they were meant to be together.

"Same with me and Cam," Elle said. "I was so freaked out by all the attention that I kept pushing him away."

Riley was flabbergasted. Sure, she realized she'd blogged about Elle a ton. But that was hardly a surprise. Elle hadn't been back to Bayside in ten years. Of course, her homecoming had been a big deal.

To hear that Elle had almost pushed Cam away because of her blogs was insane. She'd assumed they'd become a couple *because* of her gossip.

"But, in the end, you wound up together. That has to count for something." Riley could hear the desperation in her own voice.

"Why are you defending the Bayside Blogger?" Carissa asked.

Riley didn't know what made her do it or why. All she knew was that her brain turned off and her heart kicked in. These were her two best friends and they deserved to know the truth.

And maybe she really needed to tell the truth. Maybe spilling her guts would help her feel less lonely. Finally. As much as she'd been telling herself that Elle and Carissa's relationships had come between them, it wasn't the only thing. There was a big, fat elephant who was constantly present with the three of them. That elephant's name was the Bayside Blogger.

"I'm actually—"

"What?" Carissa asked.

"I'm the Bayside Blogger," she whispered so low that even she had to strain to hear herself.

"Huh?" Elle asked.

"I said…" She took a deep breath. "*I* am the Bayside Blogger."

"Get real, Ri." Carissa took a long gulp of coffee.

Elle snorted. "Seriously. She's written about you plenty."

Riley looked down at her hands. Somehow they had become tightly twisted together. She could feel the sweat on her palms. "I had to write about myself." She glanced around the coffee shop and dropped her voice even lower. "To make it more believable."

"Whatever," Carissa said with a head shake.

But Elle caught on more quickly. "You're serious."

"No, she's not." But Carissa looked from Elle to Riley and then back to Elle.

"I am. It's me. I'm her. I'm the Bayside Blogger." She went on to tell them how she returned from New York and came up with the idea. Neither she nor Sawyer had had any idea that the simple gossip column she'd pitched would turn into what it became.

When she was finished explaining, she sat back feeling like a weight had been lifted from her shoulders. For the most part, she'd been able to keep the secret with little fuss. Besides, she'd had Sawyer to talk to when she needed him. Still, there were times she'd wanted to let Elle and Carissa in.

Her feeling of calm came to a screeching halt when she saw the expressions on her friends' faces.

"Oh, Riley," Elle said, a combination of hurt and disappointment laced in those two simple words.

Carissa was worse. She was mad, extending a finger in Riley's direction. "You wrote all that stuff about me?"

"Uh, yeah," she answered quietly. "I never lied, though. All of the things I wrote were true."

"And hurtful. You told the entire town that my ex-husband cheated on me. Dammit, Riley. Do you have any idea how embarrassing that was?" Tears welled up in Carissa's eyes.

"But it brought you and Jasper together." Riley felt desperation creeping into her voice. She realized that what she'd believed all along to be a matchmaking plot might not have gone the way she'd intended—and she was about to pay a price.

"It's a lucky coincidence that Jasper and I rekindled our relationship and, trust me, it had nothing to do with you. How could you do that to me?" Carissa stood quickly, her chair toppling over. Every pair of eyes in

The Brewside turned in their direction. Riley could feel the heat on her cheeks.

"Car, please just sit back down and we can—"

"We can what? Talk? What can I say to you now that won't end up in your column?" She quickly righted the fallen chair.

"I've *never* written about anything we agreed to keep secret between the three of us. I wouldn't do that. And I never would. I keep my promises, Carissa."

One tear spilled over, falling down Carissa's face, a rare occurrence for her typically stoic friend. "I feel like I don't know anything about you anymore. I need some space." With that, she grabbed her tote bag and quickly fled the café.

Riley's heart sank. "Aren't you going to storm out on me, too?" she asked Elle softly.

Elle shook her head. "Don't get me wrong, Riley. I'm furious, too. But with me, the Bayside Blogger was more of a pesky fly. With Carissa, she was a fly carrying some disease. You really hurt her. How could you do that?"

"I don't know," she said, her voice hitching.

The truth was, keeping something of this magnitude from her two besties was brutal. Especially since she told them every other minute detail of her life.

"The whole Bayside Blogger thing just became so much bigger than everything else."

That was certainly true, but if Riley was being completely honest, being the Bayside Blogger offered her a respite from her real life. It was like a shield that she got to wear. An invisible shield that only she and Sawyer could see. By enabling her to concentrate on everyone else in town, she didn't have to think about her own life.

And how empty it really was.

She didn't have to remember how she'd spectacularly

messed up in New York. Or feel the poignant sting of her heartbreak and betrayal.

"I'm going to go check on Carissa," Elle said.

"Okay, let me know how she is."

Elle shook her head. "You betrayed my trust, Riley."

Riley swallowed past the lump growing in the throat. "Please don't be mad, Elle. Please don't hate me."

"I need some time, too. This is a lot to take in, to be honest." Elle gathered her belongings and walked out of the coffee shop, leaving Riley alone with a pit in her stomach.

What had she done? How could she fix this? Make it right?

Her own tears threatened, but she was very aware that people were still watching her. She felt naked suddenly. Was this how her friends had felt when she'd been writing about them?

"Everything okay over here?"

Riley startled at the sound of Tony's voice. His eyes were kind as he looked at her.

"Uh, yeah, of course. Carissa wasn't feeling well," Riley covered smoothly. "It came on pretty fast. Elle just went to check on her."

"Hope it wasn't anything she had here."

"Nah. She wasn't feeling great before our yoga class, either."

"Sorry to hear it. And even sorrier to say that you guys will probably be in the next Bayside Blogger column," he said.

Riley didn't have to see her reflection to know that the color had drained from her face.

"You think?" she asked.

Tony nodded. "Definitely. I don't know if she has this

place bugged or what, but seems like she always captures gossip from inside these walls."

Riley wanted to protest. She wanted to call Tony out on his statement. She got tips and leads nonstop, every single day. And the absolute biggest contributor to her site was from the man standing right in front of her. If only the rest of the town knew how many tips Tony passed on to her, his business would be cut in half.

Her phone sat deep within the shadows of her oversize purse. She didn't need to look at it to know that Tony had just sent her a message. His preferred method of communication was via direct message on Twitter.

As Tony returned to the front counter, she gathered up the remnants of their carb-fest. She was pretty sure that she'd never regain her appetite after what had just transpired with her two best friends.

Idiot. Stupid. Dumb. If she didn't write about their fight, that would be as good as outing herself as the blogger to Tony—who might out her to Bayside.

Yet how could she break a promise to her best friends?

She knew chastising herself couldn't reverse time. But, for the first time in the two-and-a-half years she'd been acting as the almighty gossiper of Bayside, she regretted ever saying anything at all.

Chapter Six

My, my, dear readers, you've been active this morning. Plenty of you witnessed something going down between Elle Owens, Carissa Blackwell and Riley Hudson at The Brewside. Unfortunately, no one seems to know just what set off the fireworks between these Bayside besties! But I do...

Sawyer was restless. He had six articles for the Sunday edition of the newspaper sitting in front of him, waiting for their turn under his final review, and for the life of him he couldn't concentrate on any of them.

He had a lot on his mind. Well, that was the understatement of the year. From saving the newspaper to his mixed-up emotions for Riley to his family's legacy and back to Riley again, his mind was overflowing with thoughts.

Leaning back, he took in his home office, his favorite spot in the house he'd purchased two years ago. It overlooked the bay and offered plenty of natural light. A large desk was set up between two picture windows. There was a cozy fireplace against one wall, and at Riley's suggestion he'd added a comfortable recliner and table in front of it.

He crossed to the fireplace now, leaned on the mantel.

The answers he sought didn't spring up from the ashes left in the hearth.

Damn.

He returned to his desk and that's when he noticed the date. Sawyer cringed. His wedding anniversary. Or it would have been if they'd gone through with it. But Rachel had called it off at the last minute.

He stretched back as far as his leather desk chair would allow. He'd been so bitter with her back then. And embarrassed, if he was being honest. Now he realized he owed her a debt of gratitude from saving them both from what would have been a huge mistake.

He'd met Rachel in college. They'd started dating junior year and it didn't take long for her to take over every aspect of his life. He'd been in love in the stupid way only a young man could be. Totally, wholeheartedly, without regard to anything besides his ever-present libido.

In essence, he would have done anything she asked.

He *did* do anything she asked.

How could he not when Rachel was so much fun? The first couple of years they knew each other, she'd been vivacious and exciting, with a love of exploring. She could turn a simple weekend into a huge adventure.

Coming from a small town where people took life slowly, Sawyer had gravitated toward her zest for life. He'd never met anyone like her. She introduced him to new cuisines and different bands and musicians. In the middle of the night, he'd wake up to her phone call and the next thing he knew, they'd find themselves in a different state. Just for fun.

After college graduation, he'd returned home and worked for his father at the *Bugle*. It hadn't taken long for Rachel to suggest they go on an adventure. She thought a move to Washington, DC, would be fun.

"Come on, Sawyer. When else are you going to have the opportunity to spread your wings and live a little? You're only young once."

It had sounded like a sound argument to him. So he'd quit the *Bugle*, abandoned his family, left his friends and moved to DC. He would never forget his parents' faces when he'd announced that he was leaving home. Quitting the newspaper.

He'd taken a job at the *Washington Post* that he hadn't particularly liked. After being the second in charge at the *Bugle* it was tough to become the small fish.

They'd lived in a tiny apartment they could barely afford. Rachel had loved it. Sawyer had been massively discontented. He was used to yard work and a big bay to swim in and actually knowing and talking to your neighbors.

But as long as Rachel was happy...

Of course, it hadn't taken long for the glimmer and shine of DC to fade away. Soon Rachel became bored with her own work as a graphic designer for a small ad firm and her wanderlust returned.

She began hinting about moving again. To New York City or Los Angeles. Yet another adventure. Only, Sawyer wasn't enjoying their current one.

He'd decided to take action. Getting engaged would fix the fissures in their relationship, or so he'd stupidly thought.

A week before the big day was set to happen, Rachel came home. She gave him one long look and admitted she wasn't happy. She was ready for a new experience. The last he heard she'd gone to live in Prague, Budapest, and at some point, she ended up in Iceland.

He guessed her explorations weren't quite over.

And Sawyer had had the pleasure of returning to Bayside, his family, his friends, and the *Bugle* with his tail between his legs and a mountain of apologies to dish out.

His parents had been saints. They'd never thrown it back in his face.

Well, Sawyer certainly had Rachel out of his system. And he had swore that he would never, ever be that selfish again.

So he'd made the *Bugle* his life. He devoted everything to it. That's why it couldn't fail now. *He* couldn't fail. The *Bugle* was his family's legacy and he'd be damned if he saw it wither away and die.

That's why he had to consider all options, including Dan Melwood's offer, no matter how extreme his demands seemed.

He reread an email exchange he'd had with the man earlier and then turned to scan the notes he'd taken during their meeting. Maybe there was a way he could convince him to move forward with his offer without bringing the Bayside Blogger into it.

Or maybe revealing the identity of the Blogger wouldn't be that horrible. Maybe Riley was sick of living a double life. Maybe no one in Bayside would even care.

His doorbell rang. Sawyer wasn't expecting anyone. In fact, he'd bailed on plans to meet Cam for some beers in order to brood alone.

He yanked open the door and sucked in a breath. Riley stood there, her red hair framing her pretty face. She wasn't wearing a coat, and the athletic clothes she sported outlined to every curve of her body. But it was her eyes that really caught his attention. The green color wasn't as bright as usual and they were puffy and red tinged. She'd been crying.

She let out a sob and he pulled her inside.

"Ri, what's wrong? Did something happen?"

He didn't even think. With one hand he shut the door while the other reached out and drew her to him, enveloping her in a hug. She came willingly, curling into him, pressing her face against his chest. She let out a long sigh and tightened her grip.

They stayed like that for a long time. Finally she pushed back. "Sorry."

"Don't apologize. Come on. I'll make you some tea."

She had no idea that he kept it stocked only for her. Sawyer despised tea.

They entered the kitchen and while he set to make the tea, she hopped up on the counter, a habit of hers that amused him. He had a table and a peninsula with three bar stools, but she always went for the counter.

"What's with the outfit?" he asked. "Pretty subdued for you."

"What?" She seemed dazed. "Oh, this. I was at a yoga class with Elle and Car—" She broke off on Carissa's name, let out a delicate hiccup.

Ah, now he was getting to it. "Did you guys have a fight?"

"You could say that." She looked down, studied her gray UGG boots.

She stayed quiet for another couple of minutes while he finished getting the tea ready. He handed her a mug and then leaned against the opposite counter. He could wait this out. Sawyer was patient. Luckily, Riley was not.

"It was a fight. A horrible fight."

"That's unusual. The three of you have been joined at the hip for the last couple of months."

She frowned. "They're my best friends. At least, they were."

"Come on. What could you have possibly done that would sever that relationship?"

Riley sighed. "I really love them. They both mean so much to me, and I would never hurt either of them. But apparently I did."

Sawyer held up his hands. "Whoa. What are you talking about?"

"We were having carbs and they were talking about much they hated the Bayside Blogger. I was shocked because I always thought I was helping them. Or, you know, the Bayside Blogger was helping them. And then…" She met his stare. "I told them I was the Bayside Blogger," she said in a fast whisper.

Sawyer gripped the edge of the counter hard so he didn't fall off in shock. "You did what? I thought we had an agreement. No telling anyone your identity." As soon as the words left his mouth he felt like a hypocrite. Dan Melwood's emails were still up on his computer in the office.

Not to mention that given the fact he was pretty sure Carissa and Elle had not reacted kindly to this news, it was doubtful that others would be fine knowing the Bayside Blogger's true identity.

"Oh, Riley," he said, suddenly feeling tired.

"I know, I know, I'm horrible." She covered her face with both hands. "You hate me now, too, don't you?" she asked between shaking fingers.

He relented. Sawyer jumped off the counter and crossed to her. Gently he removed her hands from her face and held on to them. "Ri, look at me." It took her a long moment, but finally her gaze slid up to his. He could see the moisture pooling in her eyes.

"I could never hate you. And I certainly don't hate you over this…incident."

"But you wish I hadn't told them, right?" She tried to remove her hands from his, but Sawyer held on tight.

"No. Yes. I mean, I'm not really sure at the moment. I know that I would have liked for you to give me a heads-up before you told them or anyone else."

She tilted her head, causing a piece of hair to fall and cover her eye. "So you could talk me out of it?"

He pushed the strand of hair off her face, lingering for a moment. Her hair was so shiny and silky. And despite coming from a yoga class, she smelled fresh, like a new bouquet of flowers. "I'm not sure if I would have tried to talk you out of it. But you and I have been keeping this secret for a long time now. Maybe it's been getting too hard to keep the truth from the people we care about."

It was this thing that brought the two of them together. But what if it was beginning to separate them from everyone else, too?

Sawyer met her gaze for a second before taking in her perfectly shaped nose and full lips. She was the most beautiful woman he'd ever seen. She was studying him just as intensely. Her chest was rising and falling and her mouth opened slightly into an appealing little O.

Perhaps the Bayside Blogger secret wasn't the only thing bringing them together.

He wanted to kiss her again. That's all he'd wanted to do since the last time it happened. But there was hurt and sadness in her eyes, and that needed to be dealt with first.

"How mad were they when you told them?"

She whistled. "Pretty pissed. Carissa especially. Elle was a little more reasonable. But that's Elle's personality."

"Do you think either of them will tell anyone else?"

"No," she said quickly, the loyalty to her friends evident. "Like I said, they're pissed for sure. But I think they get the repercussions. At least, I hope they do."

"Give them some time. A couple days to cool off." A thought occurred to him. "Elle and Cam are engaged. I hear Jasper and Carissa are moving in together. What if there's pillow talk and the guys end up blabbing?"

Riley's face deflated. "Oh, God, I don't know. What have I done? I'm such an idiot."

Sawyer disagreed. An idiot? No. Impulsive and often times overzealous? Absolutely. He stepped closer to her and framed her face in his hands. "Riley Hudson, you are not an idiot. You're one of the most caring, loving, smart, funny, loyal people I know. I hate when you're down on yourself."

She scrunched up her nose. "Yeah, well, I hate when I go and do something really stupid that I can't take back."

"Everyone has regrets."

"Not as many as me, apparently." She laughed lightly but there was still a hurt expression on her face.

Sawyer realized, and not for the first time, that there were things Riley was still keeping to herself. Secrets that might bring them closer if she would only open herself up to him.

He stepped even closer to her. "I wish you would talk to me, Ri."

"I do talk to you. Like, every day."

He placed a finger against her lips. "Really talk to me. Let me in."

The indecision was clear as day. It was a struggle for her. Maybe it was that, or maybe it was the fact that her eyes still held so much emotion after her rough morning. Sawyer wasn't sure. All he knew was that they were close, so close, and he gave in to his wants.

He touched his lips to hers. She inhaled a quick breath, and followed it up by lacing her arms around his neck and pulling him closer to her. The longing to feel her lips on his again subsided, only to be replaced by something much more potent. Lust, pure lust, washed over him.

His mouth moved greedily over hers, reveling in the taste of her, the smell, the touch. She made a little sound of longing in her throat and it almost undid him.

She was still sitting on the counter, and next thing he knew, he was scooping her up. She gasped when he lifted her.

"Sawyer."

He nipped at her lips. "Is this okay?"

"Yes. Oh, yes."

He didn't need to hear more than that. Somewhere in the back of his mind, he was wondering how they'd gone from her bad morning to him carrying her into the living room and gently placing her on the couch. But it was very far in the back of his mind. Right now, all he wanted was more of her.

He covered her body with his and she welcomed it with open arms that twined around him, moving up and down his back. When her fingers snuck under the bottom of his shirt, he jumped at the touch.

She giggled. He looked down at her face. She was smiling and her eyes had finally lost some of the hurt. "Is someone ticklish?" she asked with humor in her voice.

"If I remember correctly, I'm not the only one who is." With that, he ran his hand up her side. She bucked and would have jumped right off the couch if he hadn't been lying on top of her.

"Touché," she said, trying to move his hand from her sensitive spot.

But Sawyer simply ran his other hand up her other side, lightly grazing the skin under her shirt. She shuddered and he covered her mouth with his again. Soon, it wasn't about one ticklish spot or another, and their hands were all over each other, caressing every spot they could reach. Over clothes, under clothes, it didn't matter.

He trailed his mouth down the column of her throat, eliciting something that sounded very similar to a purr. Riley took the opportunity to try to remove his shirt. He shifted helpfully but, somehow, they got twisted, and the next thing he knew he was falling.

Sawyer hit the floor next to the couch with a *thunk* and before he could recover from that, Riley landed on top of him. They were both stunned, and there was silence for a long moment before they started laughing.

"Are you okay?" they asked at the same time. Obviously they were if the laughter said anything.

"Holy crap. Did we just fall off the couch?" she asked, propping herself up on her elbows and looking down at him.

"Seems like it. That's definitely a first for me. Now that was quite a kiss." He'd meant it lightly but a shadow passed over her face. "Ri, what's wrong? Are you sure you're not hurt?"

"I landed on you, remember?"

"You weigh like two pounds."

"There's a comment I'd like to hear over and over for the rest of my life."

She made to move, but he yanked her back to him. He kissed her lightly and tightened his arms around her. "Where did you go just now?"

She averted her eyes. "Nowhere."

"Don't avoid me. You gave me the same look you did back in the kitchen when I asked you to talk to me."

She bit her lip, deciding. "There are things from my past that I just don't like talking about. And when you pointed out that we'd been kissing—and of course we had—I kind of, well…"

"Freaked out a little?" he guessed.

She nodded. "You're my boss."

"But I'm also your friend."

She cupped his cheek. "That makes it worse. We shouldn't keep doing this."

He didn't second-guess himself. Instead, Sawyer went for it. "I want to keep doing this."

"You do?" Her voice was filled with shock. "Why? I mean, really? What would our parents think?"

"Ah, I really don't want to think about my parents at this particular moment."

What he did want to do was probe into that secret she was keeping from him, find out just what it was holding her back. But before he could do any of that, the door-bell rang and Riley jumped off him. She was already straightening her clothes and the couch cushions by the time he righted himself.

He took one last long look at her and decided that anything he was going to ask would have to wait. Instead, he walked to the door and pulled it open to see Cam standing there with two six-packs of beers and a grin.

"Since you refused to come meet me for a drink, I'm bringing the drinks to you." He handed one of the six-packs to Sawyer. "You're still lame for pretending to work on a Saturday."

Having hung out for years, Cam was comfortable in Sawyer's house, and he headed toward the living room. When he saw Riley, who, for her part was looking extremely guilty, he stopped in his tracks.

"Wait, were you actually working?"

At least Cam seemed oblivious to what they'd actually been doing. "We were just going over some edits on late deadlines," Sawyer lied smoothly.

"Nice work outfit," Cam said to Riley.

"I was at yoga earlier," she said, blushing.

"I'm just teasing you, Ri. But speaking of yoga, did

something happen? Elle was in a weird mood when she came home."

Riley jumped. "Um, I don't know. It was fine. I mean, um, I have to go." She pointed toward the door and then quickly made her retreat.

"Riley, wait." Sawyer gave Cam an apologetic look, handed the six-pack over, and ran after Riley, who was faster than he realized. He caught up with her in the driveway, her hand clutching her key fob.

"Sorry, Sawyer," she said. "I need to go."

"Was it Cam's question or the couch? Or the floor?"

She blew out a long breath. "All of the above?" she asked. Her face grew serious. "It's been a weird morning. I have a lot to think about."

"We both have a lot to think about. But I meant what I said in there. I don't know when or why or how this all started. All I do know is that there's something between us that I want to explore."

"But...but," she stammered. "We've known each other forever. And we've never done any of that before. I mean, except for Thanksgiving." She wiggled her finger toward the house as if that was a clear indicator of their earlier make-out session.

"Things change and I'm okay with that. The question is, are you?"

"Sawyer, I just hurt my two best friends. I need to fix that first."

"And you will. Like I said earlier, just give them some time."

She nodded firmly, although her face belied the action. She was uncertain and nervous. He got that. It had been a big morning for her.

Sawyer waited until she got in the car and watched as she pulled out of his driveway, drove down the street and turned the corner. Before heading back inside to Cam, he took a moment in the brisk November air.

The one thing that had come out of the entire day was that Sawyer had finally realized all the feelings and urges he'd been suppressing about Riley were out in the open now.

He wanted her. It was as simple as that.

Chapter Seven

Spotted: Sawyer Wallace "working" over the weekend. Only...he wasn't alone. What member of the Bugle's staff kept him company? Or, should I say, what FEMALE staffer... New couple alert? Keep me updated, faithful gossip birdies.

"Where you off to, boss?"

Sawyer halted in his tracks. He'd been trying to sneak out quietly without drawing attention to himself. His sports reporter's question had squashed that hope. Every head in the bull pen turned in his direction, including Riley's, the one person he was really trying to avoid.

"I'm just running out for an hour or so to do some errands. Carry on, everyone."

He hated acting suspicious and shady. He knew his intentions were noble, but he didn't want to share the details of his outing until he returned. Since it involved Riley and her new predicament, he'd been laying low all morning.

He could feel those gorgeous emerald eyes burning into him now. *Don't look at her. Don't look.*

Of course, he looked.

As usual, she was beautiful. She was wearing a pink sweater and had her hair pulled back in a ponytail. But those who really knew her would notice the shadows under her eyes. Because he understood what was happening in her life, he realized she'd probably spent the whole weekend fretting about the fight with her friends.

That's why he was sneaking out now.

She tossed him a questioning stare. He responded with a nod and continued out the door, zipping his coat as he went.

It didn't take long to walk from the *Bugle*'s office to The Brewside, which was great since it was a particularly cold day. The wind was biting and there was a feeling of snow in the air.

He pushed open the main door to the coffee shop, soaking in the aroma of freshly brewed coffee beans. A blast of air from the heater washed over him, warming his chilled skin.

He sidled up to the counter where Carissa was talking with Tony. "What's that amazing smell?" he asked. Besides the coffee, there was something sweet in the air.

Carissa beamed. "Just some of my world-famous cinnamon raisin scones."

"Carissa's catering company is going to start offering one specialty item every day," Tony said around a large bite of the scone.

"Want one?" she asked Sawyer, gesturing to the tray of fresh-from-the-oven scones.

"Do you really even need to ask me that?"

Tony wiped his mouth with a napkin. "So, Sawyer, what brings you in this time of day?" He looked at his watch. "You want the usual?"

"Sounds good," he said. "I'm actually here to meet with your new baker and…" They all shifted their attention to the front of the room as the door let out a little jingle. "Here's my other date," he said as Elle smiled at them and crossed to the counter.

"Dates with two of Bayside's most beautiful women,"

Tony said with a wink. "Lucky guy." He leaned across the counter. "I should warn you, though. They're both taken."

Sawyer faked shock. "Ladies, you deceived me."

"I'm making up for it with scones," Carissa said, and led them to a table near the window.

"Fair enough."

After Tony brought over their drink orders and they'd dispensed with the pleasantries, Sawyer jumped right into business.

"You're probably wondering why I asked the two of you here today," he began.

Carissa sat back in her seat. "I think we figured out the crux of it."

"You want to talk about Riley," Elle added.

He nodded and sipped his coffee.

Carissa huffed. "Riley or the Bayside Blogger? Seems they're the same person."

Suddenly Sawyer wasn't sure how to proceed. Riley had been right when she'd said Carissa was upset. Even now, there was an angry tint to her cheeks and her eyes had narrowed. But he'd decided yesterday to try and right this situation. Riley was an employee of the newspaper, and therefore he had a responsibility to try to fix this.

Hell, even he didn't buy that.

He was going to try to fix this because it was Riley.

"I can't image how you felt learning that Riley is…" He glanced around the nearly empty coffee shop. Still, he lowered his voice. "Learning about Riley's alternate identity."

"Alternate identity? It's not like she's Batman," Carissa said with a snort. "She's a gossip columnist."

"How could we have not figured this out?" Elle asked. "How does she know all the information and details that she does? We took a trip to DC together a while back and I remember that the Bayside Blogger still put out a column."

"Technology," Sawyer answered. "She can write from anywhere. As to all the details, well, let's just say that as much as the fine citizens of Bayside complain about the gossip, they sure do love to contribute to it."

"You mean, people help her write her columns?" Elle asked.

Sawyer nodded. "She gets tips and items all day long, every day. She could probably stay in her house for a month straight and still put out a column every single day."

"I still can't believe that she hid this from us. We're so close." Elle worried her lip.

"Couldn't have been easy. She came to my house after she told you on Saturday. She was a mess."

Elle seemed sympathetic to the statement, but Carissa held firm. "Oh, so sorry that Riley was distraught over something she caused. Poor little blogger." She sighed. "You don't understand, Sawyer. You're not the one she keeps writing about."

"Um, I beg to differ. Thanks to one of her items, my mom started grilling me on these imaginary girlfriends Riley threw in her column."

Elle and Carissa worked hard to stifle smiles. In the end, they both lost the battle and it didn't take long for Sawyer to join in on the laughter.

"See, it's not that bad," he said.

"But, Sawyer, you weren't dating anyone else and you're not getting engaged." She paused. "Right?"

"Of course he's not," Elle chimed in. "He wouldn't have kissed Riley on Thanksgiving if he was into someone else."

Gah. "She told you about that?"

Elle and Carissa exchanged a look that clearly read, *Duh*.

"Of course, she did, although, it's really not that surprising," Elle said.

"It's not?" he asked. "What else—"

Carissa interrupted him. "Can we stay on topic here? I went through a lot of tough times that I would have preferred to keep to myself. The Bayside Blogger didn't give me that option. She told the whole town my very personal business."

"I know she did and that sucks. But let me ask you this. Was any of the info she reported on false?"

"Huh?" Carissa asked.

"Was it gossip or fact?"

"Well, fact, I guess."

"See, Riley and I had two rules when it came to the blogger. The first was that every single item she posted, tweeted, wrote about, had to be fact. No presumptions. No lies. No embellishments. If she reported that someone cheated on their significant other, they did. When she says someone is raising havoc in The Brewside, they are."

Elle leaned forward, interest shining in her eyes. "So Mrs. Winters really did take a burlesque dance class over in Riverdale?"

"My eyes are still burning over that one, but yes," Sawyer admitted.

"What's the second rule?" Carissa asked. "Between you and Riley?"

Sawyer waited a beat, making sure he had their full attention. "That she wouldn't tell anyone her identity."

They all paused, realization settling in.

"Then why would she tell us?" Carissa asked softly.

"Because she loves you and respects you."

"And she trusts us," Elle added.

"I think she was probably feeling a little bad, too. It's a big secret she's been keeping completely to herself all this time. Couldn't have been easy. In fact, it must have been pretty lonely."

"She betrayed my trust," Carissa said, and crossed her arms.

Sawyer stifled a sigh. "You could argue that she betrayed the whole town. And that most of the citizens of Bayside betrayed one another. There's a lot of betrayal going on here."

He finished his coffee and put the empty cup back on the table. "I understand you're mad at her. I'm just asking you to forgive. Riley really loves both of you and she's devastated to realize how much she's hurt you. And I know you both love her."

Elle leaned her arms onto the table. "What about you, Sawyer? How do you feel about Riley?"

Heat washed over his face and suddenly Sawyer felt uncomfortable in his chair. "Riley and I have known each other our entire lives. She's a talented writer and a good employee. And she's my friend. She always will be."

Elle's eyes softened. "Sometimes relationships change."

If he thought he was uncomfortable before, it was nothing compared to how he felt now. "Well, I don't know that we need to…"

"Oh, give him a break, Elle." Carissa rolled her eyes. "They have to come to it in their own time."

"I suppose you're right," Elle agreed.

"I appreciate you meeting with us, Sawyer," Carissa said. "But I just need a little more time to work out how I feel about all this."

He supposed that was the best outcome he could hope for at this point. Besides, when it came to things concerning Riley he had quite a bit of thinking to do himself.

Interesting meet-up at The Brewside today between
Sawyer Wallace, Elle Owens and Carissa Blackwell. The
three had their heads together for a long time. Couldn't
catch any snippets of the conversation, but maybe it had
something to do with Carissa and Elle running out on
Riley the other day.

Riley stared at the message that Tony had sent her over
direct message on Twitter. Why in the world had Sawyer, Elle and Carissa gotten together? Of course, Elle and
Car were on friendly terms with Sawyer, but that was
still an unlikely trio.

Maybe this had something to do with how weird Sawyer had been all morning. She knew something was up
with him when he left earlier.

Riley turned her attention back to her computer screen,
but she couldn't stop thinking about Tony's message. Not
to mention the fact that, as usual, Tony had been sending
her tips all weekend and she'd yet to post any of them.

The blank Word document staring back at her was
like a big neon sign shining the word *loser* over and
over again. She had a major case of the blogger's block.
Ever since she'd spilled the beans to Car and Elle she'd
been unable to post anything other than a couple of lame
tweets. Pretty soon people would start to notice.

Since she'd spent the entire weekend moping in her
apartment with Chinese takeout and bad reality television, she took some time to go through all of the tips she'd
received. She'd have to cobble an article out of them.

She was halfway through a column about a possible
new romance between two of the teachers at the high
school when Sawyer's voice bellowed out from his office.

"Hudson. Get in here."

When had he gotten back? Must have used the back door.

Riley got up. She shook her head at the *oohs* emanating throughout the bull pen as she walked to his office, entered, and shut the door behind her.

"So?" he asked.

"So what?" She took a seat in front of him, smoothing down her black wide-leg pants, pink wool sweater and leather belt with polka dots. Her matching pink pumps peeked out from the bottom of her pants as she crossed her legs.

"It's almost noon. Where's the blogger's column?"

"Ah, I see, I knew you loved reading it."

"Riley." His voice may have taken on a hard tone but sympathy shone in his eyes. "What's going on? Is this because of what happened with Elle and Carissa the other day?"

She shrugged. "A little. I mean, it was a pretty tame weekend around here, too. Nothing exciting to report."

He leaned forward on his desk. "No tips came in from your usual sources?"

"Actually…let's talk about that." She leaned forward, mirroring his pose. "I did happen to get the most interesting tip just now."

She paused and he waited.

"Well? Are you going to tell me what it was about?"

Riley tapped her foot in a quick staccato. "Why don't you tell me, since the tip was all about you."

Confusion crossed his face, followed by awareness and a cute reddening of his cheeks. "Someone told you that I met your friends at The Brewside this morning, didn't they?"

She nodded. "Was it just a coincidence? Maybe you

went in for some of Tony's Monday-morning sticky buns and ran into Elle and Carissa?"

"Or maybe I asked them to coffee."

She frowned. "Why would you do that?"

He removed his glasses and the confused expression she thought was adorable crossed his face. "I guess I was just trying to help you."

Her heart melted. When was the last time someone had helped her? When was the last time someone had spoken up on her behalf?

Certainly not when she was in New York.

"Well? Do they still hate me?" She held her breath, fearing the answer.

"Your friends don't hate you, Riley," he responded quickly. "But they are angry."

"I deserve that." She stood and crossed to the window. Peering out at the street below, she said, "I shouldn't have told them. I can't believe I did."

"Neither can I. Riley?"

She turned back to face him.

"Why did you tell them? What made you pick that moment?"

She shrugged as if the answer was inconsequential or elusive when, really, she knew exactly why she'd spilled the beans.

She was lonely. Revealing her secret to her two best friends gave her a moment of inclusion. Of course, that only lasted a second before reality came crashing down. Now she felt even more isolated.

"I wanted to unload my biggest secret," she told Sawyer.

He saw through her words immediately. Sometimes it was like he had an insight right into her mind, as though he could edit through her thoughts to get to the crux of the matter.

"I don't think the Bayside Blogger is your biggest secret."

She crossed her arms around her stomach protectively. "Oh really? Think I have some other identity that's bigger than the blogger?"

He'd been watching her from behind his desk. Now he joined her by standing. "Yes." He skirted the desk and stopped in front of her. "I think you have a whole story from your time in Manhattan. One of these days, you'll trust me enough to share it."

Her mouth fell open. How did he know?

They stood like that, in front of his desk, only inches apart, for a long time. Vaguely, she wondered if any of their coworkers noticed them. Surely someone was watching the two of them staring into each other's eyes.

He had the most alluring hazel eyes. She'd always been able to get lost in their depths.

Eventually Sawyer broke the spell by sitting down on the edge of his desk. "In the meantime, I have a favor to ask of you."

Not what she was expecting him to say. "Okay?" she said, uncertainly.

"You know I go to the annual Technology in Print Publication Conference every year." She nodded. "It's two days from now and Bob had to back out. He has a family commitment he can't get out of."

She had noticed Bob was out of the office this week. "And you want me to go with you?"

"In Bob's place. Yes. You know how you always think of me as Superman?"

"I literally have never thought of you in that way."

He ignored her. "Turns out I can't be in more than one

place at once. There are some workshops on social media and communications I think would be beneficial to the newspaper. You're the perfect person to cover them."

Something felt fishy about this invite. She *was* the perfect person to cover anything related to social media. Heck, she'd taught most of her coworkers how to use Instagram and Snapchat. But why hadn't he asked her to go to this conference in the first place?

Unless…it was due to money.

"Sawyer, why didn't you ask me about this earlier?"

He coughed. "We never send more than two people and Bob has seniority over you." He didn't meet her eyes. "Is that a yes then?"

She ignored his question. "So we'll be going away together. Just the two of us."

He made a low, guttural sound. It was pure male and pure sex.

She knew the feeling. A couple days away with Sawyer. Alone. Despite her hesitation to get involved, she knew her resistance was wearing thin. Besides, this was for work. Her job. "Uh, I guess I can do that."

"It's a couple hours away at a ski lodge. Not sure if they have snow yet or not. But there's all kinds of things there—sledding, exercise facilities, spa, that kind of stuff. Bring warm clothes. The conference is pretty casual."

"Do I need to register or anything?"

"Um, no. Don't worry. The paper will take care of everything. Just be ready to head out early in two days."

She left his office, but stopped right outside the door. Leaning against the wall, Riley took a moment to compose herself. She would be ready for the conference. The real question was, would she be ready for Sawyer?

Chapter Eight

Ho. Ho. Ho. Anyone guess the *Bugle's* potential new couple yet? The lovebirds didn't get the memo about going south for the winter. I heard they're traveling to a swanky ski resort in the Blue Ridge Mountains. Is *conference* the new term for *tryst*?

Having Riley by his side was torture.

Especially when she smelled so damn good and looked even better in an outfit that she had deemed was "ski-chic casual" when he picked her up. Whatever that meant. One hour into their car ride and he was already having a heck of a time keeping his eyes on the road and off her. Not to mention the itching in his fingers to reach out and touch her.

For her part, Riley seemed oblivious to the frustrated attraction on the driver's side of the car. She was singing along to some Christmas song on the radio.

The truth was, he'd lied about Bob. In fact, he'd just used this whole conference as an excuse to get her out of town for a few days to clear her mind.

Clear her mind, but cloud his.

He stifled a grumble. While he might have lied about Bob, who was never supposed to attend this conference, he hadn't been completely dishonest. There would be workshops and lectures on social media. When it came to anything remotely related to the internet, Riley was the best.

After what felt like a million years, they arrived at the hotel. The Pine Ridge Ski Resort was nestled in the Blue Ridge Mountains, a couple of hours from Bayside. The backdrop was stunning. Snow fell onto the forested peaks from the cloudy sky.

The resort looked just how he'd imagine a ski resort to be. It was constructed of a dark brown wood and had a plethora of tall windows. He could see smoke rising from several chimneys and a chairlift traveling to the top of a mountain behind it.

There was actually snow on the ground already and a flurry of activity as other cars pulled in, no doubt also attending the conference. A large sign greeted the attendees as hotel employees helped collect baggage and usher the guests into the lobby.

Sawyer and Riley made their way inside the rustic lodge and to the front desk, where they waited in line for about ten minutes. Sawyer felt nerves in his stomach as he stepped up to the counter. He glanced at Riley, who was busy checking her phone. No doubt, dealing with the Bayside Blogger.

"Checking in?" The man behind the counter smiled at them. His name tag read James.

"Yes. Room under *Wallace*." He eyed Riley, who was still ensconced with her phone. Perfect. He leaned closer to the counter and lowered his voice. "And I had called about getting a possible second room."

James typed quickly on the keyboard as his eyes stayed trained on the computer screen in front of him. "Yes, I see the note here. One moment."

Sawyer held his breath. He really hoped they could accommodate his request for a second room. He'd had no problem getting Riley into the conference, although he did have to pay the highest rate for registering her so late. Still, if his libido was so out of control during one car ride, there was no telling how he'd handle sharing a hotel room. Not to mention how irritated Riley was likely to be.

He was determined to stay positive.

"Unfortunately, we don't have any spare rooms."

There went that.

"We've been booked with this conference for several months. Plus, the weather forecast is calling for snow so every other available room has been reserved by skiers and snowboarders. I do apologize."

Sawyer stifled a groan. "I understand. Do you think we can get a room with two beds at least?"

More fast typing. "Hmm. I'm not sure we can do that, either." He studied the screen. "Tell you what. Check-in is not for another couple of hours. I know the conference starts before that. Why don't you leave your bags here and see to your conference sessions? No promises, but I will do the best I can to accommodate you."

"The best he can for what?" Riley asked, suddenly appearing right next to Sawyer.

Before Sawyer could answer, James said, "A room with two beds."

Riley tilted her head in question. "We're sharing a room?" She bit her lip and appeared nervous.

"Yes, we're sold out this week," James answered helpfully.

"That's odd. What about Bob's room?"

"We don't have a reserve—"

Sawyer sprang into action. "Uh, I think that Bob canceled his reservation when he realized he couldn't attend." He sneaked a glance at James, who was watching him with an amused expression on his face. "They must have given it to another guest."

James grinned. "Exactly."

"Oh. Well, um, okay."

Was it his imagination or did Riley seem as nervous about bunking together as he was?

"James is going to do his best to get us a room with two beds." Sawyer gave the attendant the eye. "Right, James?"

James spoke up quickly as he took Sawyer's ID and credit card. "Absolutely, sir."

Riley twisted her fingers together. "It's not like we haven't shared a hotel room before."

That was true. Their families had gone on countless vacations together over the years. Of course, they were no longer kids and their parents were nowhere to be seen. This time, it would be the two of them. Alone. In a hotel room. For three days.

Suddenly, Sawyer's face felt flushed. He accepted his driver's license and credit card from James and shoved his wallet back into his pocket.

They secured their bags with the bellman and did a quick tour of the hotel. If Sawyer hadn't been feeling so anxious he would have been charmed by the high ceilings, exposed beams and countless fireplaces with comfy sitting areas. Not to mention the views of the snow-covered mountains.

They registered for the conference, received a packet and name badges, and reviewed the schedule. "I guess we should go to this first session. It's for all attendees. After that, I'm going to meet with some different vendors for our app."

"Thinking about switching?"

"I just want to see what else is out there. Can we save any money." He noticed her raised eyebrow. "Don't start."

"Fine," Riley said. "I'd like to attend the workshop on Facebook Live and videos for Twitter."

As they walked toward the meeting rooms, he could feel the tension rolling off Riley in waves. Couldn't blame her. They'd kissed twice now. Besides all of the issues Riley was having with her friends and the Bayside Blogger, she had made it clear that they really shouldn't kiss again. Well, mostly clear.

Sawyer ran a hand over his face as they found two seats and settled in to listen to the first lecture. Three days with the woman he wanted to kiss—and perhaps more—but who he absolutely should not kiss—or do more with. Great.

This was going to be the longest three days of his life.

It had been one heck of a long day.

As they rode the elevator up to the third floor, Riley rolled her head back and forth trying to dislodge the tension that had formed as she'd sat through lecture after lecture.

While most of the sessions she'd attended had actually been interesting, it had still been a lot to take in at one time.

Technology in Print Publications. Riley knew it was an important subject. Keeping up with the latest trends was important for all publications but especially for a small outlet like the *Bugle*. Hadn't she been pushing social media for years now? How many reports had she compiled for Sawyer so he could see the benefits of increasing their use?

God bless Bob for attending this with Sawyer in the past, although she didn't know how he'd managed it. Bob was an amazing writer and an even better editor. But he was very much the stereotype of the old-school news reporter. As far as she knew, he never went online. She wasn't even sure if he had a Facebook page.

At least she'd had a good time at the mandatory cocktail hour and dinner. She'd loved meeting reporters and editors from different publications. And if she did say so herself, she'd dazzled quite a few stuffy librarian-types with stories from her various experiences.

She'd told a table of freelance reporters all about the Bayside Blogger. Well, not everything, obviously. In third person, she was able to convey how popular their blogger was. And how the residents of a small town that was rather dead during non-tourist times had come alive with the opportunity to gossip about one another.

She glanced at Sawyer. He'd seemed to be in his element, as well. He knew a lot of the attendees and speakers. More, they all knew him. Even though he tried to downplay it, they'd been impressed with him.

Was it crazy that she found him even sexier than before? The way he'd taken the time to really listen to each person he spoke with. How he'd fiddled with his glasses when he was intrigued with a new idea. How he was dressed in another argyle sweater and corduroy pants that should have made him look like one of her college professors...but made him look completely sexy.

She was out of her mind.

She'd overheard more than a couple conversations praising him for sticking it out. Their fellow attendees appeared to believe that small newspapers were soon to be a thing of the past and they couldn't believe the *Bugle* was surviving.

What exactly did that mean?

She'd had a feeling for a while that Sawyer was keeping something from her regarding the newspaper. She'd even asked him a couple times, but every time she did, he'd brushed her question off.

Riley opened her mouth to ask him again, but he beat her to it.

"Did you enjoy the sessions today?"

She could tell he had. Besides the constant compliments, he'd been busy scribbling notes, eyeing different exhibits and excitedly talking to vendors.

"They were interesting."

The elevator stopped on the third floor and they stepped out into the hallway. Sawyer grinned at her. "So, tell me, could you have taught any of them?"

She held her own smile in. "Maybe. Just a few."

"Before you came along, we didn't have much of a social media presence. You really upped the bar for all the departments." His grin faded. "I hope you weren't bored today."

"Are you kidding? Social media is constantly evolving. There's always something new to learn."

He mock-wiped his forehead. "Phew."

They started walking down the hallway toward their room. "I'm here for you."

He stopped outside their room and looked at her. A crease formed on his brow, a sure sign he was deep in thought. "Yes, you are and I appreciate it, Riley. I really do."

Sawyer let them into their room with the key card and stopped in the entryway. Riley ran right into his back.

"Hey, what gives?" she asked, even as her hands lingered a little too long on the strong muscles of his back.

"I don't think you're going to be too happy but..."

He trailed off and she peered around him. "What? I

don't see any…" And it was her turn to trail off because what she did spot was a bed. A large king-size bed that certainly appeared to be extra comfy with plush white bedding and an ample amount of pillows. The operative word was *one*. One bed. As in, oh my God, she was sharing a bed with Sawyer.

Sawyer, her boss. Who she was now lusting after day and night. Night and day. Around the clock.

"Riley!"

Sawyer's loud voice pulled her out of the merry-go-round of thoughts. "Sorry, what?"

"I said, I can call down to the desk. They told us we would have two beds."

She pushed past him and walked into the room. "Actually, they said they would *try* to get us a room with two beds." He picked up the phone on the bedside table and she held out a hand to stop him. "I think we've put them through enough downstairs. They're obviously fully booked, so let's try and figure this out ourselves. Maybe they can work out another arrangement tomorrow."

Sawyer slowly lowered the phone. "You're right."

She threw her big tote bag onto the bed. "Of course, I am. Besides, we're both adults."

She didn't mean to linger on the word *adults*. But she did and Sawyer took notice. His gaze landed on her lips. He shoved his hands into his pockets, and quickly averted his eyes and looked at the bed.

Yep. They were two adults who were clearly lusting after each other staring at a big comfy bed.

Not awkward at all.

"I can always just sleep on the couch," Sawyer offered.

"No," she said. "I'm smaller. I'll fit better on a…" Riley did a quick lap of the room, which had been decorated in soothing white, beige and warm brown tones.

There was the infamous bed with two end tables. A sliding door led out to a balcony with a beautiful view of the mountains. The snow was falling faster and heavier now, reflected by the nighttime ski lights. To the left of the door was a closet and to the right was a dressing area and bathroom. She saw a little sitting area with two over-size chairs, a table and a television.

And absolutely no couch.

Well, damn.

Sawyer shook his head. "Why don't I ask the front desk if they have a cot?"

She shimmied out of her cardigan. "No."

"No?" His eyebrow arched.

"Sawyer, we have to get over this. So we made out a couple times."

He sat on the edge of the bed and studied her for a moment. "Is that all it was?"

She gulped, her throat suddenly feeling dry. Very dry. "Of course. Anyway, it's a huge bed and it's only a couple nights."

Again he remained quiet for a moment as he considered her words. "If you're sure."

"Yes, I'm sure. It's fine. Totally okay."

Since she'd known him her entire life, neither of them had ever had any problem talking to the other. They had a lifetime of conversations and inside jokes to fall back on. However, the tension in this room was thicker than the snow covering the ground.

Sawyer cleared his throat. "I think I'll just go grab a coffee."

"Sawyer, it's ten o'clock at night."

"Oh, right. I meant I'll get a decaf. Want anything?"

Yes, you. Ugh. "Um, no, I'm fine," she said as he

started walking out of the room. "I'm going to jump in the shower. I can't wait to get out of these clothes."

Sawyer stumbled and fell into the closet door.

"Ohmigod, are you okay?" She rushed to him.

She'd never seen his face—or anyone's really—quite that shade of red.

"I'm fine. I don't know how that just happened," he said, trying to right himself awkwardly.

"Here, let me help you." She grabbed onto his shirt and gave one big yank. Next thing she knew, she felt Sawyer's body launch toward hers, and they both fell against the opposite wall.

"Oomph."

Their bodies were flush together. In an attempt to break their fall, his hand had landed on her breast and her mouth was snug up against his throat. Even at the end of the day, he still smelled amazing. She tried to move her mouth to say something and her lips brushed against his skin. Sawyer shivered.

He must have realized where his hand was, and he swiftly removed it as they tried to untangle themselves. Still, they were close. So close. His warm breath fanned across her face and her lips parted.

Next thing she knew Sawyer muttered, "To hell with it," and his lips were on hers.

There was nothing sweet or subtle about this kiss. It was fast and furious and completely intoxicating. Riley heard herself groan as her fingers clenched his shirt, pulling him even closer. His mouth devoured hers.

When they finally came up for air—a minute later? Five minutes later? Who knew. They stood, staring at each other. Her chest was rising and falling as she attempted to calm down her pulse and get her breath back in check.

He searched her face, looking for something as his mouth opened and closed. Finally he pointed to the door. "Coffee."

She nodded. "Right. Shower." She inched back toward the bathroom as he slipped out of the room.

Yeah, she was definitely getting into the shower now. A nice *cold* shower.

Chapter Nine

Sawyer slept a total of fifteen minutes that night. How could he sleep longer than that when Riley's warm, soft body was lying right next to his?

When he'd returned from getting his coffee, she'd emerged from the bathroom, smelling even better than before. If that was possible.

As he'd lain in bed, his senses had been assaulted by the smell of her freshly washed hair. The lotion she'd used had a hint of lavender, which he'd always heard was supposed to be calming. Then why was his heart beating triple time?

He'd never stayed so still in all his life. It was as if moving, even to turn onto his side, would break some kind of spell. Instead, he stared at the ceiling, replaying their earlier kiss over and over in his mind.

What had he been thinking?

Easy answer. He *hadn't* been thinking.

Hence, now he was lying in this bed, not sleeping.

At some point, Riley began dreaming. She was murmuring in her sleep. Sawyer watched as she turned onto her side and curled up into a ball. His fingers were itching to reach out and stroke her hair, but he knew if he touched her, even once, he'd never be able to stop.

He had to wonder what his teenage self would think of this development. They'd always been in each other's lives, but when they were growing up, he'd never experienced feelings like this. In fact, he used to offer her advice about boys.

He remembered her first crush, a guy named Josh. She'd written him a note and they'd had a typical two-week-long junior-high relationship. When Josh dumped her for another girl in their class, Sawyer took her out for ice cream.

As he thought about the happy memory, he finally drifted off.

Morning came way too soon. Despite barely getting any shut-eye, Sawyer had never been happier for a new day to come. He sprang from the bed and hit the shower, then dressed quickly.

He peeked at the bed, where Riley remained asleep. She was on her back with one arm thrown over her face, her red hair a stark contrast to the white sheets.

He didn't want to wake her, so he scribbled a quick note and left it on the table next to her. Before he left, he took another moment to study her beautiful features. Again, the urge to touch her washed over him. It seemed to grow stronger and stronger each day.

As that thought entered his mind, he realized he had to get out of the room immediately. He made his way quickly down to the lobby.

"Good morning, Sawyer."

"Hey, Jack." Sawyer shook hands with his friend, Jack Rodger. The two had met when they worked together at the *Washington Post* in DC. Jack had stayed in the city and was now running a successful magazine. "Didn't see you yesterday."

"I got in late," Jack explained. "I couldn't make it here until the end of the day. Coffee?"

"Absolutely."

They hit the free breakfast buffet and caught up. Sawyer filled him in on the first day of the conference, the *Bugle* and Riley. Well, most of the Riley situation.

"Riley Hudson." Jack sat back in his seat, the remnants of his pancakes dotting the plate. "I haven't seen her in years. Didn't she visit you in DC when she was still in college?"

Sawyer smiled. "Yeah, took the train down from New York. That was a long time ago. She's definitely not in college anymore."

Jack studied him before a grin broke out on his face. "Oh, really?"

"What does that mean?"

"You tell me."

Sawyer groaned. "It's complicated."

Jack waited patiently. It was unnerving.

"What? We're not together," Sawyer said.

Jack leaned back, studied him. "Do you want to be together?"

He knew he should deny it, but he found himself too exhausted to resist. "Yes."

"Well, then, that's new."

Sawyer shook his head. "Not really. What's new is me acting on things I've been feeling for some time."

"What does she think of this?"

Sawyer accepted a refill of coffee from a passing waiter. "She's…cautious."

"Interesting that she's here at all, then. Last time we emailed, you said you were coming alone." He arched an eyebrow.

"It's not like that. I didn't bring her to… I mean…"

Jack's face broke out into a grin. "I wasn't implying anything."

"She's going through a rough time back home. I

thought it would be good for her to get away. Plus, most of this digital information is right up her alley. I don't know why I didn't think of bringing her before."

"Back to all those feelings you have for her," Jack said.

At that moment, his phone went off. Saved by the bell. But when he saw who was calling, he stilled. Dan Melwood was surely calling to pressure Sawyer into this deal. He shoved the phone back in his pocket without answering. "More complications."

Jack watched him with curiosity. "How about a subject change?"

"Yes, please."

"How in the hell are you making the *Bugle* work?"

Sawyer groaned. "That's part of that whole complicated subject. Fact of the matter is that…I'm struggling." He sat back in his chair and let out a long exhale. It was the first time he'd admitted out loud to anyone that the newspaper was in trouble. Surprisingly, it actually made him feel a little better.

"I'm not surprised. Small papers are folding across the country. And you're still publishing every day. Crazy. How in the hell are you doing it? More importantly, why are you doing it? Why not go down to a couple days a week?"

It wasn't like he hadn't thought of this. The *Bugle* was probably the last paper of its size to publish daily.

Not to mention, he had a tradition to uphold. The *Bugle* was his family's legacy. Each generation made it work. He refused to be the weak branch in his family tree.

When his dad had been at the helm, everyone had insisted that newspapers were dying. His dad ignored the naysayers and started the digital edition.

He'd made his mark and Sawyer was determined to

make his, too. If there was anyone in the world he wished he could emulate, it was his father.

"I'm proud that we publish every day."

Jack considered that for a long moment. "Are you sure you're not mixing pride with stubbornness?"

Jack's words shocked him into silence. That's not what he was doing. Sawyer didn't consider himself a stubborn man. And yet...

"Listen, Sawyer, you have a lot going on in your life. You want my advice?"

More like, he *needed* his advice. He nodded.

"Make some decisions. Go for it. Whether with the *Bugle* or with Riley. It's time to act."

Sawyer couldn't get his friend's words out of his head all morning. *It's time to act.*

Jack was right. Decisions needed to be made. When he returned from the conference, he had to tackle the newspaper. Right now, he still didn't know what to do about Dan Melwood. And maybe Jack was right and had a point about his unwillingness to cut the paper down to a couple days a week.

Thoughts and ideas swirled around his head. This conference was no place to make big decisions regarding work.

Riley however... He may not be able to act on his whims with work, but he could address his feelings for Riley.

It's time to act.

Again he felt bolstered by Jack. He wanted Riley. Yes, he was her boss. Yes, they'd been in each other's lives forever. But the feelings he had for her weren't going away. If anything, they were growing stronger by the day.

He didn't want to belittle her concerns, but he did want

to show her that he could be a good guy. He was someone she could trust with her heart.

So far, they'd kissed in the cold on his parents' deck
and in an alleyway. Where was the romance? She deserved more.

A plan began to form during his morning meetings.
Between sessions, he worked with the hotel staff on lo-
gistics for his plan, including keeping Riley occupied.
He knew from her text messages that she was attending
an all-morning workshop. He had the front desk find
her and present her with a gift certificate for a pedicure,
something he knew she loved to get.

While she was busy getting toenails painted, he
stopped at the gift shop and bought her two dozen roses
in a variety of colors. Sawyer didn't have any kind of
eye for design, but when the food he'd ordered appeared,
the waitress delivering it helped him set everything up.

Pleased with how it turned out, he barely had time
to take it all in before he heard the key card at the door.
Riley entered the room.

"You'll never guess what I got?" she said excitedly,
rushing toward him and showing off her bright red toenails, still clad in fuzzy spa slippers. When she noticed
the flowers and the table set with candles, she froze. "Am
I in the right room?"

"I believe so," he said.

She touched one of the roses. "Do you have a date I
don't know about?"

"Kind of."

It was as if all the air left her body, deflating her. "Oh."

"Riley," he began, but she was already inching backward toward the door.

"I'm sorry. I didn't realize... You probably know
women here."

"Riley," he tried again.

"We should have had a system. Like a hanger on the door handle or something."

"Riley!" At that she stopped. "My date is with you."

She dropped her bag on the floor and cocked her head. "Huh?"

He ran a hand through his hair. "I mean, if you want to have a date with me."

"I...well..." She peeked around him at the set table. "You did this for me?" He nodded. "Why?"

"I wanted to thank you for coming up here with me." He blew out a frustrated breath. "No, that's not the truth."

"You're not trying to thank me?"

"No. Yes. I mean, of course I appreciate you attending the conference." He gestured at the table with his arm. "But all of this is for you."

She bit her lip as she walked to the table and ran her hand across the white tablecloth. She leaned over and smelled the flowers. "First, a free pedicure and then..."

She trailed off, her green eyes growing in size. "Did *you* pay for my pedicure?"

"You deserve to be pampered every now and then."

She laughed. "Are you trying to romance me, Sawyer Wallace?"

"Yes." He didn't offer more. He wanted her to know he was serious. Needed her to know.

Her smile faded.

He stepped toward the table and began removing lids. "I wanted you to have a good dinner. Since the local options are limited and there was no dinner at the conference tonight, I ordered in for us."

She studied the dishes and her mouth formed an O. "Is that...?"

"Mac and cheese with lobster."

"Diet be damned. Holy hell, that smells amazing."

"I couldn't decide what to get with it, but I figured filet mignon goes with everything."

"Oh, yum."

Her mouth was practically watering. His eyes fastened onto her lips. They were so close, so enticing.

"What's that?" she asked, breaking his lustful thoughts.

"I ordered a special dessert just for you."

He removed the lid of a fancy silver dish with a flourish, secretly hoping the hotel had gotten his special request right. And not only because he'd paid through the nose for all of this.

Riley stepped closer. "Chocolate cake," she said with awe.

Sawyer finally sneaked a glance at the dessert. He smiled at the sight of two huge pieces of Riley's favorite treat. "Not just any chocolate cake. It's made with dark chocolate."

"You really did this for me?" she asked, wonder in her voice.

"Of course." Now he felt nervous.

As if Riley sensed it, she inched closer, a sly smile spreading across her face.

"Tell me something. If Bob had come with you instead of me, would you have ordered him chocolate cake?"

Relaxing, he grinned. "Nah. Bob's a potato-chip man."

She took another step closer and placed her hand on his chest. "Sawyer, why am I here?"

"I told you—"

"Why am I *really* here?"

Since he'd known Riley her entire life, he knew the set expression on her face. She was the most stubborn person when she wanted to be. So he relented.

"It's just that you've been going through a lot lately.

Missing your parents, being the blogger, admitting you are the blogger, your friends. I thought a couple of days away would help."

Sawyer didn't know what he expected her to do or say, and, as usual, Riley surprised him.

Tears pooled in her eyes and her lip trembled. Then she took a deep breath.

The tears never fell. Instead, she burst into laughter.

Riley could not believe she'd started laughing. She certainly hadn't meant to. She just couldn't believe what was happening, or she was completely insane. Maybe a combination of the two.

Once again, the idea of someone taking care of her and thinking about her needs was overwhelming.

And not just anyone. Sawyer. The man she could no longer deny she had romantic feelings for.

All morning, as she'd been attending workshops and lectures, she'd thought long and hard about her fight with Elle and Carissa. And she couldn't help but be reminded of all those nights in Manhattan. When she'd been surrounded by millions of people and yet had never felt more alone in her life.

It was bad enough when she found out that the man she loved was engaged to someone else. But when her coworkers discovered that she'd been dating him, they'd all turned on her.

Not one person had supported her. She'd had no one to turn to.

Her laughter abruptly stopped.

It's not like it had been her fault. How in the world was she to know her boyfriend had a whole second life? Maybe she'd just been stupid and naive.

Wasn't a person entitled to make a mistake now and then without being crucified for it?

An image of Elle and Carissa's faces when she'd told them she was the blogger flashed into her mind.

Not quite the same scenario as New York, yet she still felt that mind-numbing loneliness.

She'd almost forgotten he was there for a second. But when Sawyer scooped her up into his arms and hugged her it was, without a doubt, exactly what she needed at that moment. The special dinner and amazing dessert were an awesome mood-boost, but this hug was even better than a pedicure.

"Thank you," she mumbled against his shirt. Then she rapped a knuckle against his chest. "You're overly kind to me, Sawyer." She swept her hand out to indicate the meal he'd had delivered. "This is the nicest thing anyone has done for me in a long time."

"You almost started crying and then you started laughing hysterically, instead. If the chocolate cake didn't bring on the emotions, what did?"

"Uh…" she stuttered. "It's just that…" She couldn't bring herself to tell him.

"You know, Ri, maybe if you tell me what it is that seems to be frustrating you it might make you feel better. I might be able to help you. Because I know it has to be more than the fight with Elle and Carissa."

"I don't want you to think differently of me."

He sighed loudly. "Do you really think so little of me?"

"No, of course not."

His face was so earnest and his eyes held such patience. It undid her.

They sat on the bed and she told him everything.

"I'm a fraud, Sawyer."

"What are you talking about?"

"You know how glamorous I used to make my life seem when I lived in New York? How I would post all those pictures on Facebook and talk about how fabulous everything was when I came home for holidays?"

"Sure."

She took a deep breath. "None of it was true."

"What do you mean?"

"It was…awful." Her voice hitched. She placed her hand on her chest to calm herself. "There was nothing glamorous about my life. I think my cubicle at the *Bugle* is bigger than my apartment was."

"Most people's first apartments are pretty crappy," he said diplomatically.

"Most people don't leave their windows unlocked and return home to find their laptop, television, iPod and cell phone stolen."

He winced and then swore under his breath. "I never heard about that."

"I never told anyone." He cursed again. "I mean, I obviously called the cops. They never found my stuff. In fact, they told me I was in the wrong for leaving my window open when I lived on the first floor in broad view of the street."

"Ri…" He covered her hand, but she abruptly pushed him away.

"No," she said, taking a deep, shuddering breath. "I need to tell you everything."

He took her hand. "Okay."

"I was always so popular in high school. I got along with everyone. College was a lot of the same. Then I moved to Manhattan, and all of a sudden I didn't know a soul." She twisted her hands together. "I thought I would meet people quickly. It had never been a problem for me before. I found my job so fast that I figured I would hang with my new coworkers."

"You didn't?"

She shook her head slowly. "I was a fish out of water at that place. It was a social media company that began as a start-up and most of my coworkers had been around since the beginning. I was the youngest by at least five or six years. It was also a very male-dominated staff. And the few women were, well, kind of intense. I mean, completely brilliant and talented, don't get me wrong. But you should have seen them. They were so sophisticated and put-together. They looked like they'd just walked off the runway and found their way to the office."

"What are you talking about? You always look amazing."

"Not compared to them. These women were sitting front row at fashion week while I was cowering outside the tent wishing and hoping I could get one glimpse inside. They carried Gucci purses and I bought knockoffs down on Canal Street.

"Every day I went into that office and was reminded that I didn't fit in. Not completely." She took a deep breath. She had to in order to say this. "I felt so incredibly lonely."

"Why didn't you ever talk to me about this? Or your parents? Or anyone from Bayside?"

She'd been embarrassed. Even now, her shoulders were tensing up simply from speaking aloud her memories of that time.

"I'd wanted to live in New York my entire life. How could I ever tell anyone that it was miserable?"

She ran a hand through her hair. "Then I met Connor."

Sawyer sat up straighter, but he remained silent.

"He was thirty, which seemed so old and mature and worldly back when I was twenty-two."

His lips twitched. "Not so much anymore?"

"Nah." She slid the slippers from her pedicure off and folded her legs under her. "Instead of making friends to go to happy hours with, I ate lunch by myself every day. I was always broke so it was usually ramen noodles."

Sawyer rose, poured two glasses of wine and handed one to her. "Go on."

"Connor must have noticed I was constantly alone. I thought he was sensitive. Now I see his behavior differently."

"I'm not going to like this, am I?" Sawyer asked, his fingers tightening around his wineglass.

She didn't answer him. She had to keep going. "Connor and I started dating. At least, I thought we were dating. Turns out, I wasn't the only person he'd been dating. In fact, he was engaged to someone else."

Sawyer rolled his neck. She could hear it crack. "You never suspected this Connor guy was cheating on you?" His words came out terse.

"Never." She shook her head adamantly. "Then he was promoted in a reorganization. That new position made him my boss."

"None of your coworkers knew you were seeing each other?"

"Nope. He made a point of telling me we had to be even more covert about our relationship because he didn't want anyone to think I'd be getting special treatment because I was dating my manager. There was no policy against it—he was just worried about appearances. Again, I didn't see it for what it was."

"What was it?"

"He took advantage of the fact that I was all alone."

Sawyer rose and poured more wine in his glass before returning to the bed. "There wasn't anyone else in the office you could talk to? What about HR?"

"It was a small marketing and communications company. The president had started it out of his living room. We had an HR consultant but he didn't work in the office."

She took a deep breath. "I didn't feel comfortable talking to any of the guys. As for the women on staff, I kind of got the impression they were disgusted. Like they thought I was the new, young girl sleeping with the boss."

He hadn't said much during her story. She'd noticed a tick in his jaw a couple times, and it seemed his eyes had darkened once or twice. But she could be making up both of those things.

This was it. The only person she'd ever told the complete truth to. Not even Elle or Carissa knew about Connor.

"Who else knows about this?" he asked, as if reading her mind.

"No one."

He whistled long and low. "That's why you came back to Bayside. This is what you've been hiding all this time."

She couldn't meet his gaze.

"Riley," he urged, scooting closer.

He was judging her. She knew it. She should have kept her big mouth shut, with him and with her friends. When would she learn that some secrets had to stay hidden forever?

"I shouldn't have told you," she whispered.

"What are you talking about? I'm glad you did."

"I told you that you would think differently of me."

He sat back, studied her. "You were right. I now realize how brave you are."

Her head snapped up. "Wh-what?"

"I think you're one of the bravest people I know. Look at what you went through all on your own. I don't know how you dealt with all of that. You were so young."

"I stayed in New York until I was twenty-six. I felt like I'd aged about twenty years in those four short years."

She let out another long sigh. "Well, now you know everything. I don't have any more secrets."

His face fell, and it was as if an invisible wall went up between them.

"Sawyer?" she asked tentatively, already afraid she understood the hesitation. "What is it?"

He shifted, putting his wineglass on the end table. "It's just that…"

She knew she should give him time. Sawyer was a methodical man. He was measuring the situation.

After a moment, he spoke. "I get it now. After everything you just told me about Connor, I understand."

She had a sinking feeling. "Understand what exactly?"

"Why you don't… Why you can't be with me."

His voice held so much sadness she wanted to weep.

"That's just it," she said quietly. "I shouldn't want to be with you because I would be repeating the same mistake I made in the past." And that hadn't turned out so great. "But…" Now it was her turn to trail off.

Sawyer straightened. "But what?"

"But I want you anyway."

She sealed her words by pressing her lips to his.

Chapter Ten

Sawyer felt blindsided by Riley's kiss—but not so much that he couldn't enjoy the feel of her lips against his. The heat of her body against his.

She'd revealed a big piece of her past tonight. His heart broke for that young girl who'd been so lonely and scared. Not to mention, how she'd been mistreated by her coworkers and by the man she loved.

The idea of Riley being in love with another man made him burn. Then again, the thought of any man mistreating her had his fingers curling into a fist.

"Relax," she whispered against his lips.

"Sorry," he murmured before moving his lips to travel along her jaw, down to her neck and back up. When he nipped her earlobe, she shuddered and pulled him closer.

"More," she said, and he was only happy to oblige.

He paid special attention to one ear and then the other. Then he returned to her lips, kissing her softly, almost reverently. Her taste was so heady. It got to him in a way that nothing else ever had.

As the kiss deepened, her lips opened and he took that as invitation to push his tongue inside, gently touching hers.

As always, she smelled so good. Like fresh fruit in the middle of summer. Or maybe flowers. Hell, he didn't know. He couldn't think.

When she pulled back, he groaned. She smiled, her eyes sparkling. She had to know she was driving him crazy.

Riley reached down and curled her fingers around the bottom of his shirt, lifting it over his head and dropping it to the floor. Before he could respond in kind, she was running her hands over his chest. Her fingers circled his nipples and gently pulled at his chest hair. When she began the descent toward his pants, he knew he needed to slow things down a little or this would be a very short interlude between them.

So he went to work on her top. In true Riley fashion, she was wearing some kind of complicated, one-shoulder stretchy sexy blouse. Sighing, he tried to figure out how to remove it, but his efforts were useless. How the hell did this thing work? How had she even gotten it on?

Riley giggled. "It's easy. See?" With one fast move, she pulled off her top and stood before him in a sexy strapless lace bra that displayed her breasts perfectly.

He unsnapped the front closure of her bra, her breasts spilling out. She reached for his hand, her own shaking. He knew the feeling. Sawyer couldn't believe he was about to touch her so intimately.

She placed his hand on her breast and he was amazed at how perfect she felt. Like silk. As he ran his thumbs over her tight nipples, she sighed deeply and her head fell backward.

Sawyer leaned in and nipped at her bottom lip, then kissed her again, harder this time. He was so involved in kissing her he didn't realize she'd unbuttoned his jeans.

"Aren't we in a hurry?" he joked.

But the tender smile she gave him erased any joking. "I think we've waited long enough for this," she said.

He couldn't agree more, and he shucked his jeans by kicking them off.

Riley wrapped her arms around his shoulders and kissed him deeply, sighing as she did. His hands roamed over every inch of her.

Their kiss intensified by the second and so did his desire for her.

Then, she playfully snapped the waistband of his boxers. "Off," she said.

"Yes, ma'am." Sawyer stood quickly. But before he could shed the underwear he paused. It was a moment of realization. They'd seen each other in fancy clothes, bathing suits and even pajamas. But never before had they gone this far.

The metaphorical line between them was about to be erased. From friends to lovers.

He opened his mouth to say...he didn't know what. But Riley stood up in the middle of the bed. Even towering over him, she was still so petite.

"I'll go first." With that, she hooked her thumbs under the thin straps of her panties and slowly pulled the flimsy silk down her legs.

With the panties dangling from one finger, she stood before him completely exposed, completely vulnerable. Yet, she seemed so confident, so sure.

As if honing in on his thoughts, she threw her panties at him. He caught them, running his fingers over the soft material while taking her in. She was so beautiful.

"Your turn," she said.

His nerves were still there, but they were rapidly being drowned out by his libido. He yanked his boxers down to the floor and stepped out of them.

Then he met her gaze. There was heat in them so intense that the usual emerald color was a dark forest green.

She eyed him, taking her time running her gaze over every part of his body. It was erotic and made him even harder, a feat he would have thought impossible.

"Sawyer." Her voice was raspy. "Come to me."

He didn't need more than that.

He joined her on the bed. Skin to skin.

"Touch me," she whispered.

Complying, he trailed his fingers up her arms. She shivered. He continued by roaming over her shoulders and down her back until they rounded her bottom. He cupped it, bringing her even closer.

Her lips met his in a deep, wet kiss that knocked all sense from him. After a few minutes of exploring hands and the intense kiss, they were both breathless. He ripped his lips from hers and moved them down her throat again. Her fingers were entwined in his hair, keeping his head close to her.

Gently he laid her down right in the middle of the large bed. Then he did something he'd wanted to do for a long time. He took one of her taut nipples into his mouth, sucking, tasting. She moaned and arched her back, bringing her breast even closer. After he lavished attention on that one, he moved on to the other. Then he ran his lips over her collarbone and up to her neck.

He ripped his lips from her throat. "Ri?"

"Yes?" Her voice was raspy and her lips were swollen. It was the sexiest vision he'd ever seen.

"Are you sure?"

Was he kidding?

They were in bed, naked, limbs intertwined. She was pretty damn sure.

At the same time, she knew that Sawyer was only

asking for her. He wanted to make sure she was okay with this.

She lifted her hips, pressing them into his pelvis. "Yes, I'm sure."

"You're not nervous?" he asked.

That's when she realized that he was nervous. "I feel like I should be."

"But you're not?"

She shook her head. "Nope." To prove it, she pushed with all her might. Sawyer appeased her by rolling onto his back and taking her with him. She straddled him.

"I don't know when this started," she admitted.

"What?" he asked.

"This wanting you. I think I've been fighting it for a long time. Now that we're here, together, like this, it just feels right."

She placed her palms firmly on his strong chest and grinned.

"What's that smile about?"

She ran her hands up and down his body. "For someone who spends most of his time behind a desk, nose buried in a newspaper, you are deceptively built, Sawyer Wallace."

He offered her a look that was purely comical. Like he had no idea what she was talking about. It made her giggle.

"Now she's laughing at me," he said with a smile.

"Not for long."

She kissed him again, feeling as though she could do this forever. She loved the feeling of his mouth against hers. Loved the way he took his time. Loved how he cupped her head, making her feel so secure. Loved... him?

She reared back. Sawyer's eyes flew open.

No way. She couldn't love him. Obviously, she loved him as a friend. But…more than that?

"Ri?" he asked, confusion on his face. "You okay?"

"Sorry." She took a deep breath and did everything in her power to push that errant thought to the back of her mind. She would need to deal with it, but not now, not tonight. "Your hand hit a ticklish spot," she lied.

He relaxed. Then he sprang from the bed. Before she could wonder why, she heard the crinkling of a condom wrapper. He was back in bed in a second, towering over her. His hands were on either side of her head as he gazed down at her. The expression in his hazel eyes was so intense, so serious. She ran a fingertip along his jaw.

He kissed her again, deeply, and gently spread her legs with his knee, positioning himself between them.

"Sawyer?" He met her gaze. "Now."

Oh my. Her breath caught as he filled her.

Then he paused, peering down at her. "Are you okay?"

She nodded and sighed. "Oh yes."

He pulled out, his eyes never leaving her face. Then he pushed back in, slowly. She breathed a sigh of contentment. Still, he continued to watch her, their gazes locked onto each other. It was the most erotic moment of her life. Never before had sex been like this.

He reached for her hands, clasping them in his much larger ones. Then he pulled them above her head, securing them into the mattress. They were in the middle of the bed. Her legs were wrapped around his hips tightly as they moved together.

They continued, their bodies moving faster until they were both gasping for breath. A feeling started deep and low in her belly, trickling to the surface in the most exquisite way. She felt as though she were seeing stars, growing brighter and brighter until they appeared to be exploding all around her. The only thing she could think to do in the moment was yell out his name as her body bucked against his.

He fused his mouth to hers as she succumbed to her release. It didn't take long for his body to tense, and then he joined her on the other side.

Exhausted, she barely had the strength to wrap her arms around him as he collapsed on top of her. She was aware somewhere in the far recesses of her mind that his weight should be overbearing, but at the moment, she didn't really care. She was warm and sated, and Riley knew she never wanted this moment to end.

They stayed that way, melded together in the center of the bed, for a long time. Limbs locked around each other, breathing finally slowing down. Most of the lights were still on in the room, which ordinarily would have made her feel self-conscious. But, tonight, there was nothing awkward about this scenario.

She turned her head toward the window. The snow was falling thickly outside the window.

Finally she let out a sound. It was something between a yawn and a purr. Amused, he went up on his elbows and grinned down at her.

"What was that?"

"Shh, I'm basking."

"Sorry," he whispered. "Bask away. But in the meantime, are you cold?"

She grabbed his arms and tugged, forcing him to fall onto her once again. "Not as long as you're on top of me keeping me warm."

He nuzzled her earlobe. As he did, she felt one of his hands move down to cup her breast.

"Hey, haven't you had enough?" she said playfully.

He squeezed her breast and bit her ear. "Not even close, Hudson."

Satisfaction rolled through her body. Not to mention, pleasure. Deep, impenetrable pleasure.

Like a queen being adored, she lay on the bed and allowed Sawyer to do as he pleased. He kissed and licked and fondled. All of it felt amazing. All of it had her sighing, gasping, moaning and writhing on the bed until her hands fisted in the sheets.

Riley knew what she wanted, but they'd only just finished the first time.

"Riley, look at me."

She opened her eyes and took in the strain on Sawyer's face.

"I need you. Again."

"Already?" she asked on a strangled breath.

He nodded. "No one has ever turned me on the way you do."

"I bet you say that to all the girls."

She meant the comment to be light and funny, but Sawyer kept his solemn expression. His eyes were narrowed and lines had formed on his forehead. She knew that look. He got it when he was deadly serious about something.

"No other girls. You and only you."

Her smiled faded. She wanted to weep at his sweet and tender words, but she didn't have time. Sawyer had her in his arms and was entering her again, slowly, gently first, then faster, harder, and before she knew it, she was calling his name, her body shaking from pleasure.

Riley's eyes felt heavy and she fought to open them. When she did, she was met by Sawyer's lopsided smile. She must have dozed off. She was now wrapped in the blankets with her head cradled on his chest and his arms around her.

"Hi," he whispered.

"Did I fall asleep?"

"Mmm," he murmured against her head as he kissed her hair. "I think you were tired."

She glanced around the room. Their dinner sat untouched across the room. He'd turned the lights down, which illuminated the falling snow outside the windows.

"That's beautiful," she said.

"So are you." He leaned down and placed a kiss against her lips.

Suddenly she felt shy. "Well, that's something we haven't done together before."

"After that, I'm not really sure why we haven't." He shifted, taking her in as he did. "Ri, you okay?"

"Um…"

"Uh-oh, that's not good."

She sat up in bed, and as she did, the blankets fell away and she realized she didn't have any clothes on. Quickly she tried to cover up.

She was glad the lights were turned low because, no doubt, her pale skin was bright red.

He clasped her hands in his. "Riley, be honest with me. You don't…" He coughed. "You don't regret this, do you?"

Her answer was fast and immediate. And the truth. "No. Absolutely not." She leaned over and kissed him again.

"I can tell you how I feel," he said with a wink.

"Oh, I bet I can guess. Men, only one thing on their minds." She laughed.

"Our relationship is changing now. You know?"

Her earlier thought of love flitted around her mind,

and once again she had to push it away. It was too soon for that. Wasn't it? Besides, sex didn't equal love. And anyway, who knew where this thing between them was going to go?

She didn't want to do it, but her mind had other ideas. Thoughts of Connor and her time with him in New York had her stomach clenching and her palms sweating. She'd learned a valuable lesson from that experience. She had to protect herself and her heart.

Being with Sawyer had felt beyond amazing. But as much as she wanted to pursue the possibility of a real relationship with him, she needed to take it slow. She needed to protect herself.

His eyes held so much hope as he waited for her to answer his question. While she wanted nothing more than to throw her arms around him, she reminded herself what it had felt like to have her heart crushed by Connor.

"I think that right now… I'd really like to eat."

Despite the disappointment that crossed his face, he recovered quickly and offered her a grin.

"I happen to know where you can get some food. It's nearby and already paid for."

"How convenient," she quipped.

He rose from the bed and threw on a shirt and his boxers. He went into the bathroom, returned with one of the plush white robes and held it open for her. She allowed him to wrap her up in it. Then his arms snaked around her middle and he drew her to him. He whispered in her ear.

"Tonight was amazing. But after everything you told me earlier about your ex, well, I understand that you may need time. I'll give you whatever you need."

She turned to face him. "Thank you," she said.

Their mouths met and they stayed together for a long time as the snow continued to fall outside and she continued to fall harder for her best friend.

Chapter Eleven

Cocooned in Sawyer's strong arms, Riley slept like a rock. She woke feeling more content than she had in years.

Before she opened her eyes and let the morning in, she took a moment to consider the man beside her.

She had to admit that she'd thought of being with him before. He was gorgeous, sweet, silly, funny. Over the years, when she thought about her ideal man, it was always someone who she could laugh with. Someone who was sensitive and romantic. Someone who valued family and appreciated community.

Holy cow. She'd pictured Sawyer.

The reality of being with him so far exceeded her expectations that she could barely keep her stomach from fluttering. The way he kissed her and lavished so much attention on her… It was overwhelming.

The very real and scary thought that had filtered into her head last night came roaring back in the light of day. Love. Something Riley didn't even know how to deal with—or want to deal with, really. She pushed that scary four-letter word from her mind and decided she would contemplate what it meant later. Much later.

After an early morning spent in bed with Sawyer and a mound of blueberry pancakes, they enjoyed a dessert of something that was even sweeter than the blueberries.

Then Riley took a long, decadent shower in the spa-like bathroom. She could get used to being pampered like this.

Sawyer kissed her goodbye and headed off to his meetings. She browsed through the on-site program and picked a couple of sessions for herself.

The information was really interesting and probably useful to her career. She noticed, though, that when one of the speakers began talking about longevity in publishing Riley started to feel uncomfortable.

Wasn't that strange?

She'd always assumed she would stay at the *Bugle* until retirement—unless she moved to another city. But after her time in New York, she knew that Bayside was where she wanted to live.

For the first time since she'd started at the newspaper, Riley actually took a moment to consider the possibility of a different job. Maybe it was the first time she'd allowed herself to admit it.

Strangely, it had nothing to do with Sawyer, either. Obviously, taking their relationship to a new level changed things. But maybe a new job, a new career, would help her claw her way out of this life slump. Elle was getting married and Carissa was having a baby. Perhaps it was time for Riley to make a leap into something new and unknown, as well.

"Someone looks deep in thought."

Sawyer's deep voice pulled her out of her musings. She shook her head and offered a bright smile.

"Hey, you." She tapped him on the chest and tilted her head. "All done for the day?"

"Yep." He laid a finger to her forehead. "What caused this line to form just now?"

"I was just thinking."

"About what?"

"About…work, I guess."

At the urge to break eye contact with him, she glanced around the lobby of the hotel, which was bustling with energy. A line formed near the elevators as badge-wearing conference attendees were exiting the meeting space to return to their rooms. On the other end of the large space, she could see the hostess of the on-site restaurant rushing to seat the influx of lunchtime patrons.

"New story idea?" he asked.

Not even close. But how to say that to Sawyer?

"Something like that," she lied. "Anyway, are you hungry?"

"Nah. I had a snack during my last session. I was going to see if I could tempt you into doing something with me."

She felt her cheeks warm as an excited sensation began low in her belly. She wiggled her eyebrows. "Oh, I think you can tempt me to do something with you."

He offered her a wicked grin. "Mind out of the gutter, Hudson. That's not what I was thinking."

Damn. "Yeah, me neither," she said smoothly. "In fact, I was hoping we could go to one of these super-fascinating lectures together."

"What a great idea," he said in response to her sarcasm. "Sadly, there are no more lectures today."

She snapped her fingers. "Darn."

"Since we don't have to be at dinner until seven, I thought we could try skiing."

Riley used to love skiing, but she hadn't been in three years. It had been even longer for Sawyer.

After they were geared up and had their lift tickets, they made their way to the ski lift and rode up to the top of the mountain.

Over the next couple of hours, one thing became obvious. They were both pretty horrible skiers.

After falling more times than was humanly possible, they returned to their room and changed for dinner. Unfortunately, there would be no repeats of last night's feast of chocolate cake and cold salmon since they were dining in the hotel's ballroom with the other conference attendees.

Riley washed down her overcooked chicken with a sip of bad wine. At least the people seated at their table were interesting and conversation flowed.

Still, it was kind of hard to concentrate when Sawyer kept sliding heated glances her way.

A few hours later, they were lazing in bed with a bottle of wine that they'd ordered from room service.

"I don't want to go back home." Even she could hear the wistfulness in her voice.

The last few days had offered her a much-needed respite from life. Returning to Bayside would mean dealing with her best friends' anger and fixing that situation. It would mean returning to work, to a job that she was no longer sure she completely wanted. A job that used to be fun and interesting. And a great hiding place.

Not to mention, when she'd left a couple days ago, she hadn't been sleeping with her boss.

"No?"

She shook her head. "Not so much. Reality lives in Bayside."

"Speaking of Bayside, what happens at home? How do you want to handle this?"

She didn't need him to define *this*. He was asking about their very new relationship, so she took a moment. "I don't think we should tell anyone." At his disappointed expression—and how cute was that—she added, "Yet."

He didn't seem completely appeased by her answer.

"There's the Bayside Blogger to consider."

"If you're worried about appearing in her column, I have an in with her," he said.

"That's just it. If we were anyone else, we *would* be in her column. If someone sees us together, like this," she said, and gestured between them.

He raised an eyebrow at their state of undress.

"Well, not exactly like this. I hope no one sees the two of us naked. But, if they see us doing anything couple-y, they might tip the blogger off. Then what am I supposed to do?"

He shrugged. "Write about us."

His answer surprised her. "And you would be okay with that?"

"Yes," he answered with zero hesitation. "I want to be with you."

Her palms began to sweat. "What about work? You're my boss, Sawyer."

"You could get a new job."

He was joking, but she couldn't let it go. "A new job? Where exactly? To the other newspaper in town? There's not a lot of options in Bayside."

Sawyer collapsed back against the pillows, too. "I know it."

"If I didn't work at the *Bugle*, where would I work?" Was she asking Sawyer or herself?

Something crossed his face, but Riley couldn't explain it. It was as if a dark shadow fell over them. Even though Sawyer shrugged it off and turned the conversation to discussing a book they were both reading, Riley couldn't shake the feeling that something was very wrong.

The next morning she still sensed something was off, but then they got busy packing up their things. They attended the closing seminar of the conference and checked out of their room.

Before they could exit the hotel, they took some time to say goodbye to fellow attendees. Sawyer was talking to a man who looked awfully familiar to her. Riley ventured over to them.

"Riley Hudson," the man said. "I heard you were here."

"Ri, do you remember Jack Rodger? We used to work together."

Realization hit her. "At the *Post*. Right. It's been a long time. How are you?"

"No complaints. Unlike this guy." Jack jabbed Sawyer in the stomach.

That was strange. Sawyer had complaints? About what, she wondered. She glanced at Sawyer, but he avoided her stare.

"What did you think of the conference?" Jack asked, causing her to rip her eyes from Sawyer.

"I enjoyed it a lot more than I had anticipated. I went to this really fascinating lecture on how to boost circulation with different social media events, like contests."

"Uh-oh," Sawyer said. "Does this mean you're going to force me to do that 'take a selfie with the editor' contest again?" Pain etched across his face.

"Oh, shut up. You loved that."

Jack laughed. "Yep, same Riley I remember."

They played catch-up for a few more minutes before checking their weather apps and deciding it was time to head out.

Jack reached out and shook her hand. "Great to see you again, Riley."

"You, too." Riley began putting her coat and gloves on.

Jack turned to Sawyer and offered him a hearty slap

on the back. "Don't worry about the *Bugle*. Everything's gonna be fine."

Riley's ears perked up as she was buttoning her coat. She knew it. She'd been guessing for months that something bad was going on at the paper. How many times had she asked Sawyer about that very subject, and every time he dodged her questions.

Obviously, he'd confided in Jack. She got that the two of them went back a long time. Maybe he wanted financial advice from his old connection?

Still, why hadn't he talked to her about this? She was one of his closest friends; someone he'd known forever and a day.

"Ah, thanks," Sawyer said awkwardly, darting a worried expression in her direction.

"Remember what I said. There's more than one way to go at this juncture, even for a small-town newspaper. Give me a call if you need anything."

Riley tilted her head as Jack walked across the lobby toward the doors. When Sawyer didn't budge, she planted herself smack in front of him with her hands on her hips.

He sighed. "Just some ideas I'm considering."

She frowned. "I've asked you this before and you always manage to change the subject or avoid it completely. Is the *Bugle* in trouble?"

"All newspapers are in trouble right now."

She pointed at him. "See, that's not a real answer, either."

"It's the truth."

"Maybe. But it's not the full story." She worried her lip as she tried to find the right words. "You can talk to me, you know."

"Of course I know that. But, right now, we really need

to get on the road. I still have to stop in at the office to-night."

"I thought you said we didn't have to go back to work today." He'd already begun walking toward the door and she increased her pace to keep up with his long legs.

"*You* don't. I do." He handed the valet his ticket. "I'm the editor, Ri. I'm in charge of everything that has to do with the *Bugle*. The good, the bad, the ugly."

What in the world? His voice held a wariness she rarely heard from him. Like the weight of the world was resting on his shoulders.

She placed a hand on his arm. "Sawyer?" she tried with a soft voice.

He faced her, finally meeting her eyes.

"I told you the most personal things about me the other night. Because I trust you." She suppressed the urge to fidget. "I only hope that sentiment is reciprocal. You can trust me, too."

"I know it."

"Then what's going on?"

He opened his mouth and Riley could tell he was about to reveal what this was all about. Then his face changed, as if a shield had dropped and he'd changed his mind.

Her heart sank.

Before she could do or say anything else, the car showed up. Sawyer loaded their bags into the trunk and Riley slipped into the front seat. He adjusted the seat and the radio. Then he set the heat. Didn't matter, she thought sadly. No amount of warm air was going to heat up the cold spot in her heart.

If she was giving herself to someone else, all she wanted, the only thing she wanted, was to get that back in return. She'd bared her soul the other night, told Sawyer her deepest secret. Then they'd shared an amazing time together.

Would their relationship start and end in the bedroom? While that aspect had been nice—okay, more like phenomenal—it wasn't the only thing she wanted. What she needed was a partner who could be there fully for her, and part of being there for someone was opening up. This was something she'd never had with a romantic partner before.

When she looked at the way Elle and Cam shared everything and how Carissa and Jasper were so in tune with each other, she couldn't help feeling pangs of jealousy. She knew now that's what she wanted, too. A man to connect with in every way imaginable.

Sawyer shifted. "Ready?"

She nodded. She was definitely ready. Ready for love and passion and understanding and sharing.

Her stomach clenched at the idea that Sawyer might not be on the same page. There might always be a wall between them. Could she live with that?

They drove back to Bayside in relative quiet. Riley had a lot on her mind, the main thing being if she'd made another mistake with a man.

She glanced at Sawyer as he switched lanes on the highway, eyes focused straight ahead on the road.

Riley knew she couldn't make a mistake with him. Not Sawyer. He was far too important to her.

Chapter Twelve

Who else has been caught in the dark cloud that hangs over the *Bugle's* fearless leader, Sawyer Wallace? Didn't he get the memo that it's the holidays? Rumor has it Sawyer hasn't found a date for the *Bugle's* upcoming anniversary gala. Perhaps that's what has him so surly...

Sawyer was in a bad mood, and not only because Riley had once again written about him in her column. Although he couldn't deny her accusations about his crappy attitude.

As usual, he returned to the *Bugle* after the conference with a pile of work. Articles needed editing, bills needed paying, advertisers needed to be appeased and staff needed guidance. Everything fell on his shoulders. He couldn't imagine being out of town for more than three days.

But what a three days it had been.

Despite his less-than-cheery mood, when he thought about the feel of Riley's silky skin or the way she looked as he moved over her, it was hard to stay sour. Their time together had been beyond ideal, which was why the way it had ended really sucked.

The car ride home had been awkward, something the two of them had never experienced before. They'd known each other too long for uncomfortable silences and tension. All he'd wanted to do was reach over and stroke her cheek, ask her what was on her mind.

He hadn't done either of those things. Now, here he was wondering what she was thinking and how he could fix this situation without telling her the truth about his dilemma with Dan Melwood.

Sawyer rolled his shoulders. He'd been hunched over his computer for the better part of two hours. No, he glanced through the door of his office, out into the bull pen. No one was left. The lights were turned low and the cleaning crew would be coming through shortly.

He saved the document he was working on and shut down his computer for the night. It was Saturday and he knew damn well that he would be working over the rest of the weekend.

He walked past Riley's cubicle on his way out, stopping briefly to take in her colorful decorations. Photos lined the walls, tacked up with multicolored pushpins. Her wall calendar displayed a beautiful cherry blossom tree, the pink-and-white hues popping out. There were Mardi Gras beads hanging from a lamp shaped as a peacock, which stood next to her computer, complete with a body made of glitter and tall turquoise-and-green feathers that stuck as high as the cubicle wall. She'd left a purple cardigan on the back of her chair and an oversize travel mug on her desk.

He knew she would soon decorate for the holidays, as she did every year. Last December, she'd strung twinkly lights around her desk and put up a small desktop tree. He wondered what she'd do this time.

Riley Hudson, he thought with a long exhale. His lifelong friend and employee. She was always able to get him to have fun. Get him out of a funk.

Except, this time, the funk had to do with her.

Sawyer finished walking through the floor and exited the building. Instead of turning right to head to the parking lot and his waiting car, he automatically turned left toward the center of town. He knew where he was headed. Riley's apartment.

It wasn't only the secret that he was keeping from her that bothered him. That, he could admit to himself out here on the cold, dark street. He wasn't happy that she didn't want to return to Bayside as a couple, something he realized more each second he did want.

New or otherwise, he didn't want to keep their relationship under cover. He would have been perfectly content to announce they were dating.

Sure, he understood her point about the blogger. How could he not? Especially when he was feeling so bad about keeping the *Bugle*'s financial troubles from her. Their time away together had been a brief respite from thinking about that. But decisions would have to be made. And soon. Too many people were relying on him.

His mind was a roller coaster tonight. When he entered her apartment building, a calm suddenly took over.

He rode the elevator to the sixth floor and made his way down the hall to her apartment. When she opened the door, surprise crossed her face. Her bright eyes widened and she automatically raised a hand to check her hair.

She'd mostly avoided him since they'd returned. Or maybe he was imagining that. They'd both been busy. But it was Saturday night and he wasn't busy at the moment. Neither was she judging by the yoga pants and oversize teal sweater she wore. Her hair was pulled back in a ponytail.

"Hi," he said lamely.

"Hey," she replied. "Is everything okay?"

"No," he said automatically. Her mouth dropped open

into an O shape and he instantly regretted his answer. Even if it was the truth.

She gestured him inside. Her Christmas tree was set up in the corner of the room near the windows. It was decorated with white lights and strands of crystals and beads. The topper was a bright star with long ribbons that cascaded down most of the tree. And every single branch held a different ornament. He chuckled silently to himself because, once again, it was so typical Riley. Fun and sparkly.

"I just opened a bottle of wine. You look like you could use a glass."

He followed her into the kitchen, which was separated from the rest of the living room by a counter. Not waiting for his answer, she was already pouring him a tall glass of red.

The kitchen smelled great. Like tomatoes and onions and garlic. Something was simmering away on the stove.

She followed his gaze to the pan. "I'm making spaghetti and meatballs. Nothing special really. The meatballs are premade. So is the sauce, but I'm doctoring it up a bit."

"Looks good," he said.

"You're, um, welcome to stay. I have plenty."

Sawyer found it interesting that she was rambling. Clearly, she was nervous having him in her apartment. Another first—she'd never been nervous before.

He crossed to her and enveloped her in his arms. She was stiff for a fraction of a second. Then she sighed, molding her body to his and winding her arms around his neck. He indulged himself by running his hands up her back. He removed the elastic holding her hair and his fingers dove into all that gorgeous red hair. It smelled like flowers in the middle of the spring.

When he placed a chaste kiss on the top of her head, she shifted, tilting her head to his. Her lips were right there, tempting and alluring.

Nothing could have kept him from kissing her.

Their lips met and it was as they hadn't seen each other in a month instead of a few days.

Her fingers dug into his neck and she hung on for dear life. He pulled her in as close as humanly possible. She tasted so damn good, like the wine she'd been sampling.

A timer went off and he reluctantly loosened his grip.

She grinned, her lips swollen and her cheeks red. "Sorry about that. It's the pasta."

He nipped her bottom lip one more time and offered his own smile.

She turned, flipped the knob on the stove, grabbed two pot holders and emptied the pot into a waiting colander in the sink.

"Can I help with anything?" he asked.

"You can check on the bread in the oven. I made garlic bread to go with this."

"This is a nice little spread you got here."

She shrugged. "I needed some comfort food. There is nothing more soothing than spaghetti and meatballs. Homemade or otherwise."

He frowned. Couldn't help it. After he removed the bread from the oven and she arranged the spaghetti, meatballs and sauce on a large platter, he touched her arm.

"You're upset with me," he said.

She didn't say anything for a moment. She didn't look at him, either. He knew her well enough to tell she was working out what she wanted to say. Then her eyes flicked up to lock onto his gaze.

"I'm not upset with you."

"Then why the comfort food? What has you upset?"

"I guess I'm disappointed." She nodded for him to grab the bread and wine as she lifted the platter of pasta. After she placed it on her small dining table, she returned to the kitchen for plates, silverware and napkins.

"I had planned on eating this on the couch. But this is kind of nice. I don't use this table often."

"You're avoiding the subject."

She sipped her wine. "I know it."

"Come on, Riley. It's me. Talk."

It didn't seem that she was going to say anything, but then it was as if someone uncorked her mouth, and the words flowed out.

"We slept together and it was amazing. But that doesn't change the fact that we've been friends our entire lives. No matter what, you'll always be my friend first, Sawyer. You can tell me anything. I know you've been holding back. I know something is going on with the paper."

She took a break to scoop spaghetti onto his plate.

"Jack confirmed my suspicions and you still didn't talk about it with me. It hurt my feelings."

A huge knot formed in his stomach over that statement. "I'm sorry, Ri. I really am. It's just, you're not only one of my oldest friends, not only someone I just slept with. You're also my employee."

She blinked, waiting.

"It's my job to protect my employees."

She studied him for a long moment. Then a smile spread slowly across her face.

"Oh, Sawyer. I don't know what I'm going to do with you."

Just like that, the atmosphere of the room changed. Everything seemed lighter.

"Are you making fun of me?" he asked, half-amused.

"A little bit."

They ate their meal and chatted about a million different things. Like always. But Sawyer knew he wanted to tell her the whole story of what was happening with the *Bugle*. Needed to.

When they were finished, they cleaned the dishes together. She cleared the table, he rinsed and loaded the dishwasher. It was such an easy domestic task, and yet it felt so very right doing it together.

As he wondered if she felt the same way, she crept up behind him and placed a kiss behind his ear.

He could envision this scene playing out every single night of his life and he would be a very happy, content man.

They moved to her couch with their refilled glasses of wine. She'd turned the lights low, and the illumination from the Christmas tree cast a soft glow over the room.

They were sitting close, holding hands. The time felt right. He began telling her his dilemma.

"The *Bugle* is in trouble."

She placed her wineglass on the coffee table and leaned forward. "Tell me."

So he did.

"I understand the situation. But how bad is it?" she asked, her brows furrowing. "Like, no hopes of bonuses ever again or a cut travel budget?"

He rubbed the back of his neck. "More like we shouldn't even order supplies." This was the part he really didn't want to say out loud. "I'm going to have to lay people off."

She squeezed his hand tightly. That simple gesture meant so much to him. Her support wound through his body and warmed all the places that were cold because of what was happening in his professional life.

"The publishing industry is tough right now," he said. "Really tough."

"I know. It's a different world. The internet has changed everything."

He hesitated before speaking, feeling completely weighed down. "People are now used to getting their news and information instantaneously and often for free."

"Our online edition is doing pretty well, right?" she asked.

"Really well, actually."

"Why not switch to online only?"

He got up abruptly from the couch and crossed to the window. He looked down at the town square below them. People were moving in and out of The Brewside. Kids were gathered in front of the large Christmas tree in the town square. He used to do the same thing in high school. Congregate in the middle of town, hang out, laugh. So many things were the same, yet everything felt different now, too.

"I wonder what my ancestors would think about going to a digital-only publication?"

"I think they wouldn't have any idea what a computer or the internet is."

He barely cracked a smile.

"Come on, Sawyer. I think they would be willing to change with the times. They did leave everything they knew in Europe to venture across the ocean to come here and start a new life. Trust me, they were ready to change. You have to be willing to adapt, too."

"All I feel right now is overwhelmingly guilty."

She crossed to him, but he continued to gaze out the window. She wrapped her arms around him from behind and pressed her cheek to his back. It was such a comforting gesture.

"What in the world are you feeling guilty for?"

"For having left the newspaper after college. For moving to DC with Rachel. My parents must have been so disappointed." He shook his head.

"Sawyer, there is no way your parents could ever be disappointed in you. In fact, I remember how excited your dad was that you were working at the *Washington Post*. You're being really hard on yourself."

He shrugged. "Still, that's how I feel. Now I have to feel guilty for what I'm going to have to do to all those employees who count on me. Riley, it's the holidays. I don't know how much longer I can drag this out. I will be solely responsible for putting people out of work."

He felt her shift. Her hands grabbed his and she spun him to face her. "Sawyer, you're a good man. A really good man. And this isn't your fault. You've been holding everything together for a long time. You need to cut yourself a little slack."

"I can't. I feel responsible for every single person who walks into that building every day." He hesitated before continuing. "The thing is, I have an out. Someone has presented me with a proposal. Only I don't think I can accept it."

"Want to tell me about it?"

More than anything. She was being so patient and so kind. It was killing him not to spill his guts to her now.

"I would." He should. "The details aren't ironed out yet."

"What's stopping you from accepting?"

He looked deep into her eyes, knowing he could get lost there. Knowing that he could hurt her if he ever accepted Dan's offer. Then again, he could hurt a lot more people if he didn't. "It may not be the right thing to do."

"Maybe you should talk to your dad. I mean, he ran

the paper before you. Plus, he's crazy smart. I'm sure he would be able to help you sort things out."

"No way." He scrubbed a hand over his face. "I can't tell either of my parents about this."

She stepped back and studied him with surprise on her face. "Why not? Who better?"

"They retired and they deserve this time to relax."

"I think they would both smack you for that comment."

"Maybe, maybe not. But I can't burden them with this, especially my dad."

The newspaper had been passed down through generations on his dad's side of the family. Because of Sawyer, his dad had been able to retire early. Even though the idea of taking over an entire newspaper had scared the bejesus out of him, Sawyer had stepped up to the plate. He'd had to because he'd owed his dad. He should have never left Bayside and run off to DC with Rachel.

"What's going on in there?" she asked, running a soft finger along his temple.

"The *Bugle* is more than a newspaper. It's my family. We may not have saved lives or found the solution to world peace. But this was the Wallace contribution to society."

"Your legacy," she said with a knowing nod.

"Exactly. A legacy that is now my sole responsibility."

Again she gave a curt nod. "Then I think you should do whatever you need to do to save the newspaper and our coworkers' jobs. Really, Sawyer. No matter what."

The option before him was to either save the newspaper or save Riley. His family's legacy or Riley. All those jobs or Riley.

Now she was essentially telling him to pick the newspaper. But doing that would make him lose her forever.

* * *

When Riley had donned one of her comfiest outfits earlier and made plans with a box of spaghetti, she'd had no idea her evening would evolve into this.

She'd been surprised to open the door and find Sawyer standing there. But getting him to finally open up about his troubles meant the world to her. It showed that he trusted her. Really and truly trusted her.

She was worried about him, though. The stress he felt was palpable.

Sawyer was such a good man. He was honest and kind. He loved his family and friends. Not to mention how much the *Bugle* meant to him and how he so wanted to protect it.

Riley wished she could help. She wanted to soothe the stress line that had formed in the middle of his forehead.

Maybe there was a way she could.

She took his hand, which she was still holding, and brought it to her lips. Kissed his knuckles. Then she went up on tiptoe and pressed her lips to his.

"You are the best man I know, Sawyer Wallace. Trust me that this whole thing will work out."

"Riley—" he began, but she cut him off with another kiss.

"Shh," she whispered. "Come with me."

He didn't move. "Where?"

She smiled. "Don't you trust me?"

"You know I do."

She tugged his hand. "Come." When he finally budged, she led him through the living room, down the short hallway, and into her bedroom.

Rather than turn the overhead light on, she moved around the room, lighting the many candles she liked to keep around her room. Then she opened her laptop and set it to play soft music.

When she was finished, she turned. Sawyer hadn't moved from the doorway.

"Are you trying to seduce me, Riley Hudson?"

She shook her head. "No. I'm trying to make you feel better. Any seduction is simply a happy perk for both of us."

"I feel better just being here with you."

When he said things like that, she was filled with a tingly sensation that made her breathless and light-headed.

She held out a hand and he moved to her.

She pulled him onto the bed beside her. Their mouths sought each other, immediately fusing in an intense kiss. Following suit, their hands were moving over each other, touching, enticing, igniting fires of desire.

They rolled over and over as clothes were shed. Her breath was coming faster as her heartbeat skyrocketed.

Finally all clothes were shed and they lay on their sides facing each other. "Sawyer," she said as her fingers traveled up his side, delighting in all of his angles and curves.

"Yes?" he answered. His own hands were having one heck of a time tracing the outline of her breast.

"I have to tell you something." She bit her lip. *I love you.* It was on the tip of her tongue, but she couldn't squeeze the words out. Not yet, even though her heart was full of such love for him.

"You mean more to me than any other man ever has."

He didn't say anything, but his eyes seemed to darken. She wasn't sure if that was a good or bad thing. Suddenly feeling anxious, she blurted out, "I shouldn't have said that."

"Why not?" he asked on a half laugh.

"Because I know it's fast."

His hand moved up to cup her cheek. "Ri, it's been twenty-nine years."

When he put it that way...

"Here's something to hopefully make you feel better. You mean more to me than any other woman has. I never thought I would feel like this."

"Again?" she asked. Surely he wasn't discounting Rachel. They'd been engaged after all. "You never thought you would feel like this again, you mean."

He shook his head. "I've never felt this strongly about any woman, ever."

She leaned into his hand and he kissed her then. She gave a little push and moved him to his back. Then she straddled him. Looking down into his eyes, she smiled.

"Really?" she asked.

"Really. You have no idea what you mean to me."

And he had no idea that she'd fallen head over heels in love with him. Maybe she'd always loved him. Maybe they were destined to be together. Riley had no idea, and, instead of telling him, she decided to show him what he meant to her.

She leaned over and pulled a condom from her bedside table. Quickly she protected him. Then, raising her hips, she lowered herself onto him, slowly, so slowly. Her breath came out as one big, desirous moan. He reared up and covered her mouth with his. They were joined together in every way possible.

Then she gave him a little shove and he fell back to the pillows. She began to move, never taking her eyes off his. His hands clamped onto her hips, urging her on. She covered his fingers with her hers as she rose and fell above him.

Their bodies rocked together in total sync, their rhythm increasing with each passing second. Soon the world around her began to blur. When she fell over the edge, he was right there with her.

She collapsed onto him as his arms came around her heated body—exhausted, sated and more in love than she had ever dreamed possible.

Chapter Thirteen

Sawyer read Riley's latest blog post and stifled the urge to pop an antacid. He knew exactly who she was referring to. Of all times for her to report on Dan Melwood, this was definitely the worst.

Not that she realized that, of course.

Now he was going to have to deal with Dan, who would no doubt be displeased. Sawyer felt the beginnings of a headache.

To think he'd been having a great week. How could he not when he'd been spending every night in Riley's arms. The way her body moved, the sounds she made when her body was being devoured by his, went a far way to making his life seem better than what it currently was.

Something had changed between them last weekend. He couldn't pinpoint it. For a journalist, he was having a tough time coming up with the right words.

It was no longer the two of them hanging out as friends. And it definitely was a hell of a lot more than sex. She'd always been important to him. But now? It was as if everything revolved around her.

To celebrate getting through another work week, they'd made plans to see a movie tonight. She was still feeling apprehensive about revealing the shift in their relationship. He was still pretending to be okay with that. At least at the movies they could hold hands in the dark.

He picked up his ringing phone without glancing at the caller ID. Maybe if he had, he wouldn't have choked at the sound of Dan Melwood's voice on the other end.

"Sawyer, the time has come for your final decision. It's been weeks now and I need to know if I should move on and invest my money elsewhere."

Sawyer stifled a groan. He leaned back in his chair as he considered how to approach this. "I appreciate you giving me time, Dan. This is obviously a big decision."

"I understand that, but I'm still wondering why you aren't jumping on the opportunity for financial help when I know very well that the *Bugle* is floundering."

Leaning back in his chair, Sawyer decided to go for it. "I welcome the financial freedom your company would bring. What I'm struggling with is your very unusual caveat of revealing one of my reporters' identities."

Dan laughed. It was a bitter, almost metallic sound. "I would hardly call a gossip columnist a reporter."

"Nevertheless, I can't tell you the name of the Bayside Blogger, Dan. Journalistic integrity."

"I can appreciate that."

"You do? Great."

"Not so great for you. Without that name, I won't back the paper. Ethical or not."

A weary groan escaped Sawyer's otherwise pinched lips. "I don't understand why this is so important to you,

Dan. I know the blogger wrote about you last summer and I apologize for that."

"Damn blogger was the cause of my divorce."

Actually, his infidelity was the real cause, but Sawyer wisely chose to keep that opinion to himself.

"Again, I'm sorry to hear that. But if I give you his or her name, what exactly do you plan on doing with that information?"

"I'm not sure yet. But I'll tell you what. We're going to keep talking in circles here. You have my proposal and all the numbers and projections. I will be at the Dumont party tomorrow night for the one-hundred-and-fiftieth anniversary of the *Bugle*. I expect an answer there."

With that, Dan disconnected. Sawyer rubbed a hand over his face. Initially, he'd been thrilled when Lilah Dumont offered to throw the *Bugle* an anniversary party. Of course, he knew Mrs. Dumont was on board with any party, any time, but it wasn't like he had room in his current budget to celebrate, and one hundred and fifty years was a long time. The entire town apparently thought so, too. He'd seen a recent guest list and it looked like everyone would be there. Despite the current financial climate—or maybe because of it—his reporters and staff had earned the right to a night of celebration.

One hundred and fifty years. Something to be proud of. Again Sawyer thought about his ancestors. What would they think knowing the Wallace family had continued their legacy?

More importantly, what would they think knowing he was screwing it up?

Sick of feeling powerless, Sawyer turned to his computer. Whenever he needed help sorting through an issue, he always wrote out each and every detail. Then he would sit back and study the list. Make a pros-and-cons list if necessary. He would do the same now. He started typing Dan's initial proposal, but then was interrupted by a question from one of his editors.

He would get back to it, though, because he was determined to figure out the best course of action. He wouldn't let his family down.

Even though the day was overcast, with thick gray clouds biding their time before they unleashed what was sure to be a huge amount of rain, to Riley it felt like the sunniest of mornings.

Something was different between her and Sawyer since he'd stopped by last weekend, and she could no longer pretend that their relationship was some kind of fluke. They were together as more than friends, more than coworkers. He was her boyfriend, and she was—she gulped—in love with him. Definitely, irrevocably in love.

She sat at her desk, unable to contain the grin at that thought.

"Do I even want to know what that look is for?" Claudia asked as she sidled up to Riley's cubicle, leaning over the edge and peering down at her with an amused expression on her face.

"Hmm? Oh, it's nothing. I'm just in a good mood today."

Claudia eyed her for a long moment. "Oh, really? I know that expression. If I had to guess, I would say you're dating someone."

"I might be," Riley replied coyly.

"It's not like you to withhold info. Who is he?"

Riley opened her mouth and quickly shut it. She couldn't exactly tell her supervisor that she was sleeping with the big boss.

"You know, I think I want to keep it to myself a little bit longer."

Claudia's face softened. "Oh, Riley."

"What?"

"You really like this guy, don't you?"

More than like. She loved him and she was having a heck of a time keeping that to herself. She wanted to shout it from the roof of the *Bugle*. Maybe take out an ad.

Her stomach took a huge dive and Riley knew she was lucky to be sitting down, or else she'd be on the floor.

Big, fat raindrops began to fall against the window and Riley suddenly understood why she'd been thinking it was sunny earlier. Because she was in love with Sawyer and she hadn't felt this good in a long, long time. Since she had dated Connor…

That thought made her sit up straighter.

Claudia leaned closer. "Okay, I feel like sixteen different emotions just crossed your face."

"Um…"

"I'm not going to push you on this guy because I'm happy for you. But you know what's interesting? The Bayside Blogger hasn't picked up on this yet. You and your new man must be really stealthy for her not to write about you."

"Uh, yeah, we've been pretty discreet." She quickly looked away.

"Hey, boss," Claudia called out as Sawyer made his way out of his office.

Riley glanced up. Sawyer tripped over a garbage can. He looked really out of it. He removed his glasses, which was a good thing since they were on crooked anyway. His mind was definitely somewhere else.

She knew how worried he was about the state of the *Bugle*. They'd spent every night together, eating dinner, watching television, making out. It had been one of the best weeks of her life. Just the two of them, enjoying each other, laughing, kissing. Maybe he was feeling relaxed because he hadn't mentioned the financial trouble again since he'd finally told her about it last Saturday.

In fact, he'd looked relaxed all week long at work, too. He'd joked around with their coworkers and brought doughnuts in almost every morning.

Now those shadows had returned under his eyes. There was definitely something up today.

"Ready for the big anniversary gala at the Dumonts' tomorrow?" Claudia asked.

The expression on his face was enough to make Riley laugh. It was as if Claudia had asked him to cut off his own hand.

"Come on, Sawyer," she said. "It's going to be fun. It's not like we have to do anything, either. Mrs. Dumont took care of everything."

"I still have to put on a tux—again—and go be social."

"Maybe Riley will bring her new boyfriend."

Sawyer's head shot up at that. Riley could feel the heat on her cheeks as she studied her desk, suddenly finding her mouse pad extremely interesting.

"Riley has a new boyfriend?" Sawyer asked, amusement in his voice.

"Yep," Claudia said. "It's serious, too."

Sawyer propped his elbows on the top of Riley's cubicle wall. "Oh, really? How do you know?"

"Because she won't tell me who he is," Claudia said, oblivious to the fact that she was talking to Riley's new "boyfriend."

Sawyer rubbed a hand over his chin. "That *is* serious."

Riley rolled her eyes and stuck her tongue out at Sawyer. "Claudia also pointed out how incredible it is that the Bayside Blogger hasn't written anything about my new relationship."

He met her gaze for a long, intense moment. She knew he was remembering her words about the blogger. Anyone else would have been busted by now. Another reason to keep their dating under wraps.

"You're lucky," Claudia said, oblivious to what was passing between them. "And I'm happy for you. About time you found a nice guy. He'd better be treating you right."

"He's...not bad," she said slyly.

Sawyer snorted.

"Has he, you know, stayed over yet?" Claudia asked, her eyes gleaming with curiosity.

"You know, he has. Although, I have to admit, he snores."

Sawyer straightened. "He does not."

Riley stifled a giggle as Claudia swiveled toward Sawyer. "And how would you know if he snores or not?"

Sawyer shoved his glasses back on his face. "I'm just saying that it's unlikely Riley would know if this guy snores because...well, um..."

"Yes?" Riley asked helpfully, enjoying Sawyer's discomfort.

"Because you always fall asleep so early," he finished lamely.

"Nice save," she whispered.

Luckily, Claudia seemed oblivious. "By the way, thank you so much for all of your New York suggestions, Riley."

Riley smiled. "Did you and the hubby have a good time?"

"It was wonderful. I've always wanted to visit at Christmastime." She glanced down at her watch. "Oh, shoot. I didn't realize the time. We have that budget meeting in a couple minutes."

Sawyer groaned.

Claudia laughed. "Did you get the latest numbers I emailed?"

"Darn," Sawyer said. "I left them on my desk. But I want to run to the restroom before the meeting."

"I'll grab them," Riley offered, popping up. "I need to get that story you edited for me anyway."

"Thanks, Ri."

As she moved from behind the cubicle, Sawyer lingered, allowing his hand to brush against her arm. It was the lightest of touches that shot a surge of awareness through her system. Her breath caught in her throat.

"You're welcome," she whispered. She desperately hoped no one detected the breathy quality to her voice.

But Sawyer did. He grinned and winked at her. Riley made her way quickly across the room and stepped into Sawyer's office.

She crossed to his desk and found her article. Her nose crinkled as she took in all of the red-pen markings. Another editing job by He Who Loved the Red Pen.

Scanning the rest of the large desk, she located the budget numbers from Claudia. As she reached for them, she bumped the mouse and Sawyer's computer sprang to life. She couldn't help but read the words that filled the screen. It was an email from Dan Melwood to Sawyer.

Riley's mouth dropped open. Holy smokes. Dan was offering to become an investor of the paper.

She wanted to throw her fist in the air in triumph. This would solve all of the *Bugle*'s financial problems. She felt so happy for Sawyer. He must be ecstatic.

But as she continued to scan the email, the hair on the back of her neck stood up.

In exchange for financial backing, the terms of which are laid out in attachment 3, the investor shall retain the right to full disclosure and transparency, including employee salaries, bonuses and legal names.

She reread that paragraph three times. What did he mean by legal names? It wasn't like anyone used a pen name. After all, they weren't writing fiction or some salacious novel or…

A secret gossip blog. *Oh no.*

Riley froze, her breath whooshing out of her as if someone had punched her in the gut. She didn't know how long she stood there, staring at the computer screen, willing it to morph into something else. At some point, the papers in her hands fell to the ground.

Try as hard as she might, every time she reread Dan's words, they were the same.

Sawyer was planning on outing her as the Bayside Blogger to get help with the *Bugle*. He was going to sacrifice her anonymity to protect the newspaper.

And why did Dan even need to know she wrote the blog? Why did he care? But, most importantly, how could Sawyer do this to her?

Once again, she wasn't important enough.

Not to mention that she knew Sawyer had been talking to Dan Melwood for a couple weeks now. This whole thing must have been planned even before they went to the conference. Before they became lovers.

A wave of nausea passed through her. She had to put a hand on the back of Sawyer's desk chair to steady herself. He'd been talking about this before he slept with her.

A sound slipped out from between her clenched lips. It was a pathetic whimper as she realized that he had no regard for her. How could he?

"Ri, what's taking so long?"

She snapped to attention when Sawyer spoke from the doorway. Seeing him brought about two very different emotions. Anger and sadness. She didn't know which one of them to focus on.

Anger won out. Big-time.

"How dare you?"

"What?" His gaze swept over her face in question.

She pointed at the computer screen. "This."

In two strides he was across the room. She put a hand up to halt him before he moved around the desk. Instead, she started reading.

"'The investor shall retain the right to full disclosure and transparency, including employee salaries, bonuses and legal names.' Sound familiar?"

He crossed the room and pulled the blinds so they wouldn't have an audience.

Sawyer pointed at his computer. "That's not what you think."

"Really? Because I *think* Dan Melwood offered you financial help and part of the agreement is revealing that I write the Bayside Blogger column."

He ran a hand through his hair. "Okay, that's pretty close. Dan does want to become an investor—"

"But what?" she interrupted. "How could you even consider this? You made me a promise when I first started doing this that it would stay between me and you."

"You told Elle and Carissa."

Her mouth fell open. "You can't compare me telling my two best friends with this." She pointed at the screen, once again reading the hurtful words typed there.

Sawyer started skirting the desk, but she moved to the other side of the room. "Riley, please?"

"Please what? Please get on board with the whole town

finding out I've been gossiping about them for years? Why does he even care?"

"Apparently you wrote something about him that pissed him off."

Her chin jutted out. "I never write anything that's not true. You know that."

"Of course."

She glared at him. "You were going to humiliate me, Sawyer. And after everything we—you and I—we've been together." A pained expression marred his handsome face, but she didn't care. With a sweeping of her arm, she tried to encompass all of the people on the other side of the door. "What would they have thought? They're my coworkers and they respect me. You know I've already been through a bad situation with coworkers. And with a guy." Her voice caught on that.

"This isn't the same situation as what you dealt with in New York."

"No? Because it's feeling pretty damn similar. Man I lo—" She stopped herself just in time. Sawyer didn't deserve to know her true feelings. Not now. "The man I like sells me out."

He stepped toward her. "Riley, it wasn't like that. I mean, it wasn't going to be. I hadn't made any decisions yet. Not really."

She threw her hands into the air. "Oh, well. You hadn't definitely decided to rat me out." She crossed the room and got in his face. With her index finger, she poked him in the middle of the chest. "But the fact that you even considered it is more than enough."

"Riley, please," he repeated, the desperation evident in his voice. He grabbed her finger, pulling her hand so her palm was flat against his heart.

"You were going to tell the whole town that I'm the

Bayside Blogger." Tears were welling up in her eyes. She took a long, deep breath, willing them not to fall.

"Dan offered me a proposal that would save the entire paper. It would keep me from having to lay off staff."

She tried to free her hand, but he hung on tight. "Save the paper at the expense of my reputation. I trusted you."

"Ri…" No other words came out. Just one syllable of her name in a weak, defeated voice.

"I thought that after this last week, things had changed between us."

"They had. This week has been amazing."

She couldn't agree more. That's why this hurt so much. "You opened up to me. You told me so much. What I don't understand is why you didn't tell me about this. Were you just going to let me be blindsided?"

The expression on his face was all the answer she needed.

Again. Just like Connor in New York. That thought was enough to have her yanking her hand away from him. Riley needed space and she needed it now.

"Sawyer, I can't."

"You can't what?" As she retreated toward the door, he followed. "Don't leave. Not like this. We need to talk about this."

She stopped when she reached the door, but she didn't face him. She couldn't. So, as she looked at the fake wood paneling of the door, she gathered herself.

"There is no we. There is no us."

"Riley," he muttered.

But she didn't listen. She wrenched the door open and left without looking back.

Chapter Fourteen

Janna Goldsmith @JGolds
Hey @BSBlogger—everyone is wondering why Riley
Hudson ran through the square with tears in her eyes.
No less than 100 people saw her. Got the deets?

Riley quickly weaved her way through the cubicles of
the *Bugle* and flew out the front door.

All she knew was that her heart was breaking and she
wanted to crawl into a deep, dark hole and hide for the
rest of her life.

She ran across the town square, bypassing The Brewside, and made a dash for the door of her apartment building.

Huffing and puffing, she got out of the elevator on her
floor and headed to her apartment. When she reached it,
she pulled up short, a gasp escaping her lips.

Elle and Carissa were standing outside her door.

"Wh-what are you doing here?" she asked through a
strangled breath, which at this point was half sobbing.

"Riley, what in the world happened?" Carissa asked.

All she could do was cry harder at the questions. At
seeing her two friends who she'd missed so much.

"Oh, Ri-Ri, come on." Placing an arm around her
shoulders, Elle urged Riley forward. She gently took

Riley's key from her hand and opened the door. All three of them entered the apartment.

Riley moved to the couch and sank down. Exhausted. Spent. But, to her disgust, the tears wouldn't stop.

She curled up into a ball and let herself cry.

All she could think about was the deep hurt and betrayal she felt. In the distance, she heard Elle say, "That's it. Let it out, honey."

She had no idea how long she stayed like that, scrunched up on the couch with her eyes firmly shut. When she finally did open them again, she had been covered up with a blanket. Elle sat on the other end of the couch and Carissa was in her oversize chair. There was a box of tissues on the coffee table in front of her, as well as a mug of what smelled like her favorite tea, a bottle of wine, a glass of water, a jumbo bag of potato chips and a box of cookies.

She sat up, adjusting the blanket around her. "What's all this?" Her voice was scratchy. Had she cried herself to sleep? "Did I fall asleep?"

Elle nodded. "For about an hour."

Carissa gestured to the coffee table. "We didn't know what you would want so we tried to cover all bases. There's ice cream in the freezer, too."

"I don't have any ice cream. I haven't been to the store."

"I went for you. You're stocked up now," Carissa said, and quickly looked down at her folded hands.

"You did?" She was overwhelmed. "Why?"

Carissa scooched forward. "Because you were upset."

Elle wrapped a hand around Riley's foot and shook it. "Because we love you."

It only took a moment for more tears to surface.

"No, no, no more crying. At least not for a little while," Carissa said.

"But I ruined your lives by being the Bayside Blogger and here you are being so nice to me."

Carissa and Elle exchanged a glance. It seemed like they were silently saying, *You go first. No, you.*

Finally Elle relented. "You didn't ruin our lives, Ri."

Riley sneaked a peek at Carissa.

Carissa sighed. "You didn't ruin my life. But I was pissed at you."

"I know," Riley said.

"We've wanted to talk to you for days, but you disappeared on us. I called the *Bugle* and they said you and Sawyer went off to a conference. After you got back, we just didn't see you anywhere."

She'd been too busy hibernating with Sawyer. Playing house. Only that had turned out to be a big fat lie.

Carissa cleared her throat. "We missed you, Ri."

She wanted to weep but for an entirely different reason. "Really? I missed you guys so much. And I'm so sorry that I didn't tell you about the Bayside Blogger. And I'm sorry I wrote about you. Really, truly, I didn't mean to hurt you in any way. Please forgive me."

"I do," Carissa said.

"Me, too," Elle agreed.

Then the three of them piled onto the couch for a long group hug. Riley felt lighter than she had in weeks. Well, until she remembered Sawyer and what she'd found on his computer earlier.

"Now that that's settled, want to tell us what got you so upset?" Elle asked. "When we saw that tweet about you running through the square crying today, it was clear that something horrible had happened.

She nodded. "But, first, I think I'll take some of that ice cream. What kind did you get?"

Carissa laughed as she rose and walked toward the kitchen. "Mint chocolate chip, cookie dough and basic chocolate. Which one do you want?"

"Yes," Riley said firmly.

"All three it is."

Not bothering with bowls, Carissa brought all three cartons and three spoons to the couch. After they'd each sampled the different flavors, Riley finally began to tell them her story. She started with her time in New York and didn't stop until she'd revealed everything about her short relationship with Sawyer.

When she was finished, she collapsed back against the couch cushion, taking the carton of mint chocolate chip with her.

"Um, wow," Elle said.

"Wow is right," Carissa agreed. "I don't even know where to start."

Riley shoved a huge spoonful of ice cream into her mouth, reveling in the minty chocolaty goodness. "We could start with how I'm an idiot. How I continue to fall for the same kind of guy who is intent on making me into a total fool."

"You're not an idiot," Carissa said loyally. "And I don't get why you think you were the foolish one in New York. You didn't make a mistake there. That lame-wad Connor did. How were you to know that the guy you were seeing was a two-timing bastard?"

"But I…" She paused. "My coworkers wouldn't talk to me and…"

"Your coworkers sound horrible. Why in the world would they blame you for that situation? Couldn't they see you were the victim?"

Elle piped up. "Not when Connor got to them first. Still, pretty shortsighted and judgy of them, in my opinion."

"Totally."

Hmm, she supposed her friends had a point. All these years she'd been blaming herself. She'd felt so disgusting thinking she'd dated an engaged man that she never stopped to admit that she'd been the victim in the situation.

Sawyer had tried to point that out, though.

Just thinking about him made her stomach clench. She still couldn't believe what she'd seen on his computer that morning.

"You're right," she told her friends. "That situation wasn't my fault. But it still happened and it was still a pretty awful time in my life. And that leads us to me coming home with my tail between my legs and working for Sawyer."

"And then doing other things with Sawyer," Carissa said with a wink. "I wish we could spill the dirt on the sexy times. More reason for me to be mad at Sawyer for ruining that, too."

"Sawyer didn't deny it when you spoke to him this morning?" Elle asked. "He really considered outing you to this guy."

Hearing it out loud made Riley want to cry. She fought the urge to grab the ice cream again.

Carissa looked perplexed. "I still don't get it. I know Sawyer. He's one of the kindest men on the planet. Why would he be willing to reveal your identity and cause you that much pain and embarrassment?"

Riley sucked in a breath as she tried to decide how much to tell her friends. In the end, she knew she needed their opinions.

"I get why."

"You do?" Elle asked, astonishment on her face.

Riley nodded. "The *Bugle* is in financial trouble. Sawyer has been faced with the possibility of laying off employees."

Suddenly she remembered her conversation with him. She gasped and her hand flew to her mouth as realization dawned.

"What is it?" Elle asked.

He'd hinted at this offer. Hadn't he told her someone had presented a way out but he didn't want to take it? She racked her brain to remember the details of that particular conversation. Sawyer had said there was something holding him back from accepting help. And she'd encouraged him to take it anyway.

As of today, he still hadn't said yes to Dan. For her.

"He loves me," she whispered.

"Hold on, everybody. The merry-go-round just made a sharp left," Carissa said. "What is this now?"

He was going to protect her over the entire rest of the staff. "I'm such an idiot."

Elle scratched her head. "I have to admit, I'm no longer following, either."

Riley quickly filled them in. "Don't you see? The *Bugle* is his family's legacy. He can't let it fail."

"So what are you going to do now?"

Buoyed by a new determination, Riley rose.

"I'm going to help him."

Simone Graves @SimGrav
Come on @BSBlogger. We're dying. What's up with Riley Hudson?

Bayside Blogger @BSBlogger
Rumor has it everyone's favorite Manhattan wannabe is

having career trouble. Will Riley be jumping the *Bugle's* ship soon? Stay tuned...

Sawyer read Riley's response to the Twitter question and let out an exhale.

What did he expect? Did he honestly think she would answer with the truth? That she would reveal that someone she'd trusted her entire life had just broken that confidence for an easy way out of a bad business situation?

His head started pounding for the hundredth time that day. Every time he thought about Riley he got a lump in his throat. Riley had never returned to work that day. Not that he could blame her.

He had sat through a boring budget meeting, two different editorial sessions and a phone call with the printing facility. If someone offered him a million dollars he couldn't say what had happened in any of those meetings.

It was dinnertime, but he wasn't hungry. Sawyer was fairly certain he wouldn't be able to eat again. The idea of putting food in his stomach made him nauseous.

He's left a message for Riley and tried texting her twice. But she wasn't answering.

So he left his house and drove over to his parents'. Despite the darkness, his dad was outside hanging Christmas lights.

A huge green wreath with a red bow hung from the front door, and candles glowed from every window. It was such an inviting and friendly scene.

Too bad it was the exact opposite of his current mood. A bad mood brought on by his own stupidity.

He threw the car in Park in front of the house, got out and slammed the door hard. His father paused with lights wrapped around his arm to eye his son.

"Hey," Sawyer called out as he walked up the front walk. The word came out terse and unfeeling.

"That's some greeting," his dad, Henry, said. "Did you have a bad day?"

Sawyer kicked at a pebble.

Henry unwound the lights and placed them on the porch. He stepped toward Sawyer.

"Today sucked," Sawyer admitted.

Henry nodded. "I'm putting these up for your mother." He gestured to the lights.

"Kinda dark," Sawyer said.

"As your mother would say if she wasn't at the grocery store. She told me to start earlier. Sometimes she's right. Don't tell her I said that."

Sawyer simply grunted.

"I could use a break. Come on."

Sawyer followed him through the house. His dad snagged two beers from the fridge and, despite the chilly temperature, they made their way onto the deck.

The water was choppy, mirroring Sawyer's mood. The air held a distinct crispness. It smelled like snow, something Sawyer really couldn't describe but knew intimately from growing up here.

They sat in silence for a few minutes, drinking their beers. Sawyer didn't mind the cold. It was cooling off the anger he had toward himself.

"So, son," Henry finally said. "What brings you here?"

Sawyer decided to get right to it. "You always say I can come to you with any problem at the newspaper? Well, I have a problem. A huge problem. And I really need your advice."

If his dad was surprised at his bluntness or the reason for visiting, he didn't show it. Instead, he nodded for them to start walking.

They descended the steps of the deck and strolled slowly around the rim of the bay, and Sawyer told his father everything. How the paper had been losing money and subscribers. About his feelings for Riley. At first, he could barely look at his dad as he revealed how he'd fallen hard for his lifelong friend. He explained Dan Melwood's proposal and what had transpired with Riley that morning.

When he finished, he stopped walking and waited for his dad's remarks, unsure of how he was going to take all this news.

To his shock, his dad threw his head back and laughed.

"Well, gee, thanks for the sympathy and support, Dad." He took a long swig of beer.

"Sorry, sorry." He continued laughing for a few more moments before pulling himself together. "It's just that… well, that was quite a mouthful."

"Tell me about it."

"Our little Riley is the Bayside Blogger." He laughed some more. "Your mother had guessed that a while ago. I told her she was crazy."

"Mom is pretty intuitive."

"Now that I think about it, I guess it makes sense. But what's more interesting…you and Riley."

Sawyer cringed. He was hoping his dad would focus on the business and newspaper portion of the story. He should have known he'd go right for Riley. "It's weird for you, isn't it?"

"Are you kidding me? Your mother and I have been waiting for the two of you to sort out your feelings for years."

Sawyer felt his mouth drop open.

"Aw, I see you're surprised. Well, I'm not. There has always been something there between you."

Fascinated, he simply stared at his dad. "How did you know?"

"Intuition. Experience. The fact that you never take your eyes off her when she's in the room with you." He rapped Sawyer on the chest. "And she doesn't, either."

Henry continued. "I always thought the two of you were perfect complements to each other. Always reminded me a little of me and your mother. Riley is the only person who can make you laugh when you're in one of your serious moods. And, likewise, you have that ability to calm her down when she becomes frenetic."

Really? He couldn't believe it. He wondered how long that had been going on. He wanted to ask his dad but couldn't get the words out. Not after their fight this morning.

"Yeah, well, it doesn't matter anyway. I really messed it up. She'll never trust me again."

"Poor kid. That must have been really hard for her to read on your computer."

"Not making me feel better, Dad."

"Answer me this. Were you really going to out Riley to Dan Melwood?"

"I don't know. I've been trying to talk him out of it."

"Why does he want to know her identity so badly? Who cares?"

"She wrote about him last summer and it didn't sit well with him. Apparently her article contributed to his marital problems."

"I don't think the words of a small-town blogger could really have that much effect on someone's marriage. There were obviously problems to begin with."

Sawyer nodded. "I agree completely."

"Plus, if you did tell him, there's no way to control who he would pass the information to."

"Again, I agree."

Henry threw his beer bottle into a recycling can as they started making their way back toward the house. He scrubbed a hand over his face in the same way Sawyer often did.

"She's written about a lot of people in this town. I can't see any of them punishing her for it and I get the feeling that's what this guy wants to do."

"I would never let that happen," Sawyer said passionately.

"You already have your answer, son."

"I do?"

"This Melwood guy sounds like a real prize. You don't want to get into business with someone like that."

"But, Dad, he could save dozens and dozens of jobs. I love Riley, but I can't put all of those people out of work for her."

"You don't have to."

"The newspaper has been in our family for a century and a half. I already failed it once when I abandoned it for DC and Rachel."

"Stop that." His father rarely raised his voice, so when he did Sawyer took notice. Just like now. "This guilt has been going on for long enough."

"But, Dad, you can't rewrite the past."

"Neither can you."

"You and Mom were so upset when I told you I was leaving Bayside for DC. I'll never forget your faces."

Henry groaned. "We were wrong, Sawyer."

"To be upset?"

"I'm not going to lie to you. It was hard for us to see you leave, to know that you didn't want to stay here and follow my exact footsteps. It wasn't long after you left that I realized how unfair that was. How much I would have hated it if my dad had done that to me."

Sawyer was dumbfounded. He didn't know what to say.

"You were twenty-two, Sawyer. So you went and worked in another city. So you made the wrong choice with a girl. You're hardly the first man to follow your—"

"Stop, Dad!" Sawyer let out an exasperated laugh.

"It's true. Rachel was gorgeous and you were young. You found your way back. What's more important is that you found your passion. Even if that passion had been in a completely different field, your mother and I would still be proud of you. So stop beating yourself up over that time in your life. You're doing an amazing job with that newspaper during a really tough time in publishing."

"Yeah, real boss-of-the-year material."

"Don't make me hit you upside the head."

Sawyer grinned because the likelihood of his dad ever hitting anyone was about as plausible as finding an envelope full of enough cash to save the newspaper.

Still, maybe his father did have a point. He'd been carrying this guilt around with him for so long. He'd always felt he'd messed up all those years ago. As long as the newspaper was doing well, he felt he was making amends for leaving his family.

"Dan Melwood gave you a great idea. An investor. That's all you need to find."

Sawyer groaned. "It's not the first time I've thought about an investor. But, Dad, how many people out there would be willing to back a small-town newspaper? Newspapers are dying."

"A fact that continues to make me sad, but that's the way of the world. You are approaching this problem from the wrong angle."

"What do you mean?"

"If you really want to save the *Bugle*, and, remember, your mother and I are okay if you don't, you need to find an investor. But not for a newspaper. Why not try searching for someone who wants to back the town." He tapped Sawyer on the head. "Think about it. And if you want even more of my advice?"

Sawyer nodded.

"Cut the paper down to a couple days a week. With the online edition, there's no need to print seven days a week. Make those issues you do print special."

"You would be okay with that?"

"It wouldn't matter if I wasn't." He rapped Sawyer on the chest. "You are the boss. And, yes, I've been waiting for you to cut back for some time now."

"Dad, you're a genius."

"Why don't you mention that to your mother next time you see her?"

"Will do."

They started walking back up the stairs to his parents' deck.

"Now, you just have to realize one more thing." Sawyer paused, waiting for his dad to reveal it. "You said you loved Riley back there." He grinned.

He did? Wow. He did.

"I, uh, well, um…"

His dad clapped him on the back. "Keep repeating that over and over. In the meantime, how about you help me finish hanging the Christmas lights and stay for dinner?"

"I can do that."

Henry slapped his son on the back. "And next time you have problems with the newspaper or problems with a female or problems that involve both the newspaper and a female, don't wait so damn long to come talk to me."

* * *

Sawyer had left no less than five messages for Riley the night before. After dinner with his parents, he'd almost gone over to her apartment, fully prepared to grovel, and grovel hard. But Cam and Jasper had shown up unexpectedly at his house with beer, cigars and a homemade chocolate pie from Carissa.

Somehow he had the feeling that Elle and Carissa had put them up to it. They'd insisted that they'd heard he'd had a rough day and wanted to help him take the edge off.

He'd called Riley once more, only to get her voice mail yet again. Then he'd stayed inside with his friends and moaned about his own stupidity.

The next morning, he drove to the *Bugle* offices and parked in his usual spot. His plan was to go over the Sunday edition of the paper, just as he did on most Saturdays. Once he was satisfied that everything was in good shape and ready for the printer, he'd head to Riley's apartment and wouldn't leave until she agreed to talk to him. Even if it took all night and they both had to miss the big anniversary party.

He entered the quiet office and flicked on some of the lights. Pausing at Riley's cubicle, he looked around once again at her funky, personable decor and the realization hit him deep in the gut.

He loved her.

He loved every last inch of her. From her bubbly attitude to her over-the-top outfits. He was head over heels for his best friend.

Sawyer continued to his office and found his proof of the paper in the middle of the desk, where his deputy editor always left it. As usual, he began with page one and barely glanced up until he'd been over the entire thing.

When he flipped to the last page, he was surprised to see another page underneath.

"What's this?" he asked into the silence.

He scanned the page briefly until he saw Riley's name at the bottom. It was a letter addressed to him.

He read through slowly, taking in every word. He could practically hear her voice saying them.

A resignation letter.

"Oh, hell," he muttered.

His heart rate accelerated as he read over the letter again, but the words were still the same.

Riley was leaving him.

She felt it was time for her to make a fresh start. That while she'd loved her experience at the *Bugle* she needed to look for new opportunities.

His palms were sweating as he put the resignation letter back on his desk. He'd really messed up this situation.

He rose and began pacing his office from the windows to the door and back again. The smell of the disinfectant the cleaners used permeated his senses. He desperately wished it was Riley's sweet scent surrounding him instead.

Had he lost her forever? Was their friendship over as well as their romance? He knew he'd blown any chance of working with her, not even in her secret role as the Bayside Blogger.

The hair on the back of Sawyer's neck stood up at red alert. A nagging feeling washed over him and all he could think about was the Bayside Blogger.

He rushed to his computer and logged in to the back end of their website. After a quick search he saw the saved article for the blogger page. It was set to publish soon.

Opening it, his eyes scanned the contents in shock.

She was outing herself.

There, in the black font that distinguished the blogger's column from all the others, was Riley admitting her true identity. As all of her articles were, it was well written and concise. She talked about how much she loved Bayside and her friends and family. She'd only meant to help and, on occasion, offer small pushes—and here she'd included her favorite winky emoticon, and Sawyer had to roll his eyes despite grinning)—to play matchmaker for couples she believed could use a little extra nudge to get to their happy ending. She'd never, ever meant to hurt anyone's feelings.

Sawyer sat back in his chair and removed his glasses. He ran a hand over his tired, weary face.

He grabbed her resignation letter again and located a particular line. *I know the* Bugle *will be fine now.* Yes, it would, if this blog posted. Riley was exposing the blogger so Dan Melwood would offer him the money and backing he needed.

She was being completely selfless. For him. And he hadn't done a thing to deserve it.

A feeling of love so strong and so visceral surged through him.

This was the polar opposite of Rachel. In fact, this was the opposite of him. He'd thought of himself when he'd left Bayside with Rachel. And he'd been thinking of nothing but himself since he'd returned.

Riley was thinking of him.

Moved beyond words, he was helpless to do anything but stare at his computer screen. After a few minutes of deep reflection the answer he needed came to him. It was so simple really.

He wasn't going to let Riley do this. He couldn't. Instead, he was going to step up and be the man she needed. A man who would actually protect her. Unlike that idiot in New York she dated, Sawyer planned to defend her to the last word.

Chapter Fifteen

This is it, Dear Readers. My moment of truth. I know you've all been dying to meet me. Well, tonight your wish is granted. The *Bugle's* anniversary party just got a heck of a lot more interesting. After all, it's not every day you get to unveil a real live gossip darling! Who do you think I am? Big hint: I'll be the one wearing the very sheepish expression…;)

Elle and Cam gave Riley a ride to the *Bugle's* anniversary party. Ordinarily, when she pulled up to the Dumonts' impressive mansion, she took a moment to take in the beauty of the estate. The classic architecture of the house, the immaculate grounds and well-tended gardens always made her sigh. Tonight she was in no mood to enjoy their lush beauty.

Instead, she began running toward the grand foyer. Well, as much as her three-inch heels would allow. It was more like stilted power walking.

She hadn't even put her usual time and attention into her outfit. She'd grabbed a vibrant purple dress that she'd worn to another Dumont party a few months back—gasp. She'd left her hair loose and kept her accessories to a minimum. In her mind, she might as well be at the grocery store.

But, after her article had published earlier in the day,

all hell had broken loose in Bayside. She knew when her revelation article posted. Not only because she'd scheduled it, but when any of her blogs went live, an automatic tweet was sent out letting her readers know.

Today, as usual, she started getting replies to her tweet almost immediately.

No way!

Is this a joke?

OMG! The Bayside Blogger is out. Do you believe it?

No way that's the Blogger? No freaking way.

At first, Riley wanted to hide. Skip the party and bury herself under the blankets on her bed until the holidays were over and it was a new year. Or, maybe forever.

But, in the end, she knew Sawyer would be here and she desperately needed to talk to him. Hiding wasn't the answer. This wasn't New York all over again. She'd run away that time. Returned to Bayside like a scared little ingenue.

Time to face the music. As if on cue, the band began playing a song. She walked into the house and was greeted by a waiter offering champagne. She ignored him and the alcohol and quickly made her way through the atrium and out the French doors to the attached tent. This party was set up just as it had been for Elle and Cam's engagement party, with heated tents, food stations and pop-up bars. Plus, a dance floor in the center of the area.

She scanned the party, her eyes searching for any sign of Sawyer. She spotted Carissa and Jasper. Carissa was waving at her frantically, but she ignored her friend, making a quick round of the tent instead.

When she was positive Sawyer was nowhere to be found, she paused. Riley had to admit that this wasn't what she'd expected. After revealing her secret identity today, she thought she would have people coming up to her left and right. Some would be curious, but some might be angry.

She even had all kinds of excuses ready to go. She was prepared to apologize profusely.

But, as she stood in the middle of the dance floor, not one person approached her. She didn't even receive the questioning glances she'd anticipated.

What is going on?

Before she could follow that train of thought, an out-of-breath Carissa grabbed her arm. "Damn, Ri, you're fast."

"Sorry. I'm just looking for Sawyer."

Carissa nodded, her eyes holding understanding. "Of course. I just can't believe he did that."

"Right. Wait, what?" For the first time, Riley gave Carissa her full attention. Carissa looked lovely. Riley didn't know if it was the simple black dress or the early stages of pregnancy, but Carissa was glowing. "What did Sawyer do?"

Carissa opened her mouth, a questioning expression on her face, but no words came out. "You don't know?"

Riley frowned. "Know what? What are you talking about?" An uneasy feeling crept up her spine.

"Oh, my God, you have no idea. Where have you been all day?"

"I've been… Carissa, come on." She shook her head, her hair landing over her shoulders. "What are you talking about? What did Sawyer do?"

Carissa grabbed Riley by the arm and pulled her off the dance floor and toward a quiet corner of the tent. "He said he was the Bayside Blogger."

Riley could feel her eyes widening even as she became light-headed. "Excuse me?"

"A blog posted to the *Bugle* site this afternoon."

She began blinking in rapid succession. "I know. I told everyone that I'm the Bayside Blogger."

Carissa shook her head. "No, Ri. The blog said that Sawyer is the Bayside Blogger."

Riley whipped her phone out of her gold clutch purse. Quickly she scrolled through the replies she'd received from Twitter. Now it all made sense. She'd thought those responses were a bit…off.

She looked up, met Carissa's expressive gaze. Carissa held out her phone. "Here, read it."

Riley took the phone in her unsteady hands and read the words she hadn't written. The blog was short and sweet. At the end, Sawyer revealed that he was the Bayside Blogger. He was the one who had been reporting on the residents of town. He stressed that he hadn't meant to hurt anyone's feelings, pointing out that every blog, every tweet, every word, had been truthful.

He'd covered for her.

He'd protected her.

He loved her.

The realization hit her harder than having every single person at the party throw their smart phone at her head. Sawyer was in love with her. Unlike her last boyfriend, he'd stepped in to shield her from pain and embarrassment. Instead, he'd sacrificed himself for her.

"Oh, my God, Carissa," she whispered to her friend as she handed her phone back.

"I know," Carissa said. "Pretty unbelievable."

Riley didn't know what to say. Luckily, she was saved by the murmur of the crowd, which was becoming increasingly louder. She and Carissa both glanced around until they saw the source of the whispers. Sawyer had just stepped into the tent.

Her breath caught. The man she loved. Her oldest friend. Her everything.

She felt a light push against her back. "Go," Carissa whispered in her ear.

Riley made her way toward Sawyer. As she did, she couldn't miss the speculation of the other guests.

Sawyer Wallace is here. Or should I say the Bayside Blogger.

I don't know. I just can't see him being the blogger. I mean, our blogger.

Why would he say he's the blogger if he isn't?

I kinda never wanted to know the identity of the blogger. Not really.

As she got closer, Riley increased her speed, even though her heels were not a fan of this decision.

"Hi," she said.

"Hey," he replied.

They stood like that, staring at each other as if they'd just met three seconds ago instead of twenty-nine years. He said, "Listen, Riley."

At the same time, she uttered, "Sawyer."

They both laughed awkwardly. He opened his mouth, but she put a hand on his arm to stop him.

"No, please let me go." He nodded and she continued. "I... I, um..."

"Riley?"

She took the deepest breath of her life. It did nothing to settle her nerves. "I love you, Sawyer," she blurted out. "And you love me, too."

The first expression to cross his face was shock. It was followed quickly by realization and then a large smile. Her favorite smile of his. The one that was slightly lop-sided and made him look mischievous and handsome at the same time.

"That's right," she said. "We love each other."

He pushed a hand through his hair, messing up the tidy style he'd attempted for the party. She loved that, too. "I knew you and I were going to have a talk tonight, but I didn't think this is how it would start. I'd assumed I would begin by groveling and begging your forgiveness."

"Oh, you can still do that."

He chuckled. "Trust me, I plan to. Because I really hurt my friend."

She nodded. "Yeah, you did."

"See, I considered doing something that would have devastated her."

"True." She stepped closer to him. "But the thing is, I get it."

"You do?" His voice was filled with surprise.

"I understand. The *Bugle* is your legacy, your family, your...thing," she supplied for lack of a better word. "If outing me is all it takes to get the help the newspaper needs, I understand."

"But in the end, I couldn't let you sacrifice yourself."

She wound her arms around his neck and stared into his amazing hazel eyes. "I wanted to help."

"I couldn't let you do that, Ri."

He tilted his head and their lips met in a sexy, soul-ful kiss that made its way through her entire body until Riley felt like she was glowing with love.

When they broke apart, she sighed. "Sawyer, I can't believe you changed my blog."

"I found your resignation letter. I knew that there was

more to it, and when I checked your blog… You are the most selfless person I know and I love you, Riley Hudson."

If she thought she was glowing before, she now felt like she was flying. Hearing the words *I love you* from his lips was too much. It was more than she'd ever hoped for.

"I can't believe you told everyone you are the Bayside Blogger," she said. "I can't believe you did that for me."

He grinned. "Allow me to repeat. I love you, Riley Hudson." Then his expression grew serious. "I don't want you to leave the newspaper," he said.

She'd known this conversation was coming, one way or another. It was never going to be easy, but now that they'd finally admitted their true feelings, it was even harder.

"I have to leave." She put a finger to his lips when he was about to protest. "It's time, Sawyer."

He appeared to take that in, thinking deeply about her words. "Are you not happy?"

She bit her lip. "I am happy at the *Bugle*. But I'm not content. Does that make any sense?"

"How long have you been feeling this way?"

She couldn't keep the sign from escaping. "I'm not sure. I think it's been coming on for a while. It has nothing to do with you or this Dan Melwood situation. I went through something horrible and crappy in New York, and instead of sticking up for myself, I ran away and came home. You gave me a job at the *Bugle* and I hid behind it. Not just as the supersecret blogger in town. But you made me feel safe."

He cocked his head. "Isn't that a good thing?"

"It's a cowardly thing. I'm twenty-nine years old. It's time for me to try something new and exciting, no matter how scary that might be."

He nodded slowly before a smile gradually lit up his face. "I'm proud of you, Ri. But I'm really going to miss seeing you and your outfits every day."

Again she twisted her arms around his shoulders and kissed him soundly on the lips. "I think you're going to be seeing me and my outfits on a daily basis anyway."

"Good. I couldn't imagine not having you in my life every day."

Nor could she.

They leaned in to seal their new arrangement with a kiss, but were interrupted by a loud cough. Together, they turned toward the sound.

Dan Melwood stood there, a cocky smirk on his face.

"Sorry to interrupt," he said, not looking sorry in the slightest. "But the time has come, Sawyer. Tell me, who is the *real* Bayside Blogger?"

Sawyer held in the groan that desperately wanted to slip through his pinched lips.

He'd stepped into the Dumont party with anxiety and fear that he'd lost Riley forever. Now, after she'd admitted that she was in love with him, he considered himself the luckiest man on the planet. It felt like everything in his world was right.

But Dan Melwood's interruption reminded him that one thing was still very not right.

The fate of the *Bugle*.

"I gave you until this party as a deadline. Do we have a deal or not?" Dan asked.

Without thinking, Sawyer faced Dan and angled his body so he could shield Riley from this pariah. To his surprise, she joined him at his side, linking her hand with his and facing Dan head-on. It was a bold statement and one that set his pulse racing. They were partners now.

As if reading his mind, she squeezed his hand and then whispered softly, "We're in this together."

"Come on, Sawyer. It's time to make some decisions," Dan said with little patience. "I told you I needed an answer by tonight. What's it going to be? Feel like saving your family's newspaper?"

He really was conceited. Sawyer couldn't believe he'd even considered this proposal or working with this man.

Over the last couple of days, and particularly the last twenty-four hours, he'd been replaying the events of his life. Of course, he felt guilty for leaving his family and his town to run off to DC with Rachel. But after talking with his dad, he decided to give himself a break. It had been one moment in time. In the end, he had done what was right. He had come back home.

While he may have contemplated Dan's offer for a moment, in the end, it wasn't right, and not only because of Riley. Sawyer loved the *Bugle* and he loved Bayside. Dan Melwood was right for neither.

It was going to be hard and it was going to take sacrifice, but Sawyer was determined to save the paper no matter what. If Riley could be brave and branch out to another job, another career, then he could figure a way out of this mess.

Still, he decided to play with Dan a bit more.

"Why, Dan, you must not have been online today. I do believe the Bayside Blogger revealed himself."

Dan rolled his eyes. "Oh, please. You're no more the Bayside Blogger than I am." He inched toward Sawyer. "Tell me who it is, really."

Sawyer wasn't going to be intimidated by this guy. He stepped forward, as well, ready to defend Riley, his newspaper, his town. Two little letters, *n* and *o*, hovered on his lips. But before he could get them out, the music stopped, and he found himself and everyone else in the tent turning toward the small stage.

Lilah Dumont was standing there in all her regal glory. She thanked everyone for coming, as she always did at these things. Then she went on to talk about the *Bugle* and how it meant so much to the community. Her husband, Collin, joined her and reiterated her thoughts, adding that he was well aware newspapers were a dying breed and how he couldn't be happier that the *Bugle* was surviving. If Sawyer wasn't radiating with such irritation over Dan, he would have been beyond touched.

He would have also noticed that Dan had moved away from him and Riley. In fact, he'd made his way to the stage. Next thing Sawyer knew, Dan took the microphone from Mr. Dumont.

"Hi, everyone," he said to the crowd. "The name's Dan Melwood. I lived here in Bayside for a few years and graduated from Bayside High."

"What's he doing?" Riley hissed.

Sawyer shook his head as the two of them moved closer to the stage. "I have no idea, but my suspicion is that he's up to no good."

They continued to make their way through the crowd as Dan began talking again.

"I am happy to be here supporting the *Bayside Bugle* tonight. Happy one-hundred-and-fiftieth anniversary." He raised a glass and most of the crowd did the same.

"However," Dan went on, "Mr. Dumont is right. Newspapers and most print media are going the way of the VCR, cassettes and floppy disks. In fact, I recently learned that the *Bugle* is in serious financial trouble."

Sawyer froze in his journey toward the stage. Riley ran into his back before coming around his side and reaching for his hand again. The crowd let out shocked sounds at Dan's admission. The whispers started up immediately.

Back at the stage, Dan waved his hands to settle the noise. "I know. Believe me. When I found out that the *Bugle* is barely able to pay its employees, well, I simply couldn't believe it."

"Is that true, Sawyer?"

Sawyer turned to find Jim and Ted, two of his reporters with worried expressions. Bob was right behind them, looking concerned.

"Newspapers are struggling all over the country," Riley said.

"I certainly know that," Claudia said, "but I didn't realize we were one of them."

Bob took a long swig of his beer. "I didn't want to think it. How naive."

Dan coughed into the microphone to get all of the attention back on him. "I know it's scary and unsettling to hear these things about a long-running and respectable institution like the *Bugle*. But don't worry. There is hope. There is a plan. At least, I hope there will be." His gaze shifted, searching the crowd until he found Sawyer. The look Dan offered was equivalent to checkmate.

"Sawyer, why don't you join me up here?"

Sawyer stifled a groan. Riley stood next to him, unmoving.

"Come on, Sawyer. Don't be shy. I know writers tend to be introverts." Dan offered a little laugh. "Let's give Sawyer Wallace, the fearless editor of the *Bugle*, a hand."

That's how he wanted to play it? Fine. Sawyer had taken his share of turns at chess. He made his way to the stage as his fellow citizens applauded. The clapping grew even louder when he stepped onto the stage.

Sawyer crossed to center stage and stood next to Dan.

"Sawyer has been doing his best to keep the struggling newspaper afloat and I commend him. But I told you not to worry. That's because I have a plan. A business plan."

He went on to relay his bio in business and all of the deals he'd made over the years, but Sawyer tuned it out. Instead, he searched and found Riley's supportive gaze. She nodded.

"I offered Sawyer Wallace complete financial support to save the *Bugle*."

The crowd roared its approval. He even heard a *hip hip hooray*.

Sawyer perused the audience. He knew almost every person in attendance. From former teachers and classmates to his employees and friends, it felt like each person contributed to his life in some way, no matter how small.

He loved Bayside. It wasn't just a town. It was a community. They looked out for one another. When someone was down, they all pitched in.

Maybe they did like their gossip a little too much, but didn't all small towns? He smiled.

His dad was right. There was another way out of this mess. And it was staring him in the face right now in the form of every person in the heated tent in the Dumont family's backyard.

He stepped up to the microphone. It was time to put his town to the test. If they responded the way he anticipated, Dan Melwood wouldn't stand a chance. It was Dan's turn for checkmate.

"It's true," Sawyer said, flinching at the sound of his voice echoing throughout the tent. "Dan did offer me a proposal to save the newspaper. It was tempting, let me tell you."

"What do you mean?" someone called from the crowd. "Are you not going to accept it?"

Sawyer paused for a long moment. He saw his parents standing off to the side of the stage. Both of them were smiling at him. His dad nodded. He definitely wasn't letting them down now.

"Here's the thing. This help came with a stipulation. Dan offered to bail out the *Bugle* if, and only if, I revealed the identity of…the Bayside Blogger."

Everyone had been quiet while he spoke; now they became even more hushed. Like they were all holding their breath.

"You said today that you were the Bayside Blogger," someone said.

Sawyer nodded. "That's right, I did."

Dan grabbed the microphone. "Sawyer Wallace is not the blogger. He lied. He is protecting the real blogger."

Sawyer didn't need a microphone. He raised his voice. "Maybe I am. Maybe I'm not. But Dan wanted a name and he got one."

Dan stalked across the stage, baring his teeth. "I'm offering to save the newspaper. All I want to know—all I deserve to know as a silent partner—is the real identity of the Bayside Blogger."

"Not at the expense of journalistic integrity," Sawyer's dad called.

"Please. We're not talking about some international headline in the *New York Times*. This should be a no-brainer. Who is the Bayside Blogger?"

The crowd was reacting exactly as he'd anticipated. They didn't like being cornered any more than he did.

But what he hadn't expected was to see Riley walk onto the stage. His heart dropped.

She took a deep breath and faced the town. "I'm the Bayside Blogger."

Chapter Sixteen

She didn't look at Sawyer. She didn't need to. She could feel him staring at her with his mouth hanging open. As soon as she'd stepped onto the stage, his eyes had darkened.

But she needed to do this.

"Sawyer is not the Bayside Blogger."

Sawyer pivoted toward her. "No, Ri, don't," he whispered.

"I am. It's been me the whole time. I'm the one who's been writing about all of you."

A hush fell over the crowd. Every pair of eyes in the house was trained on her. Riley gulped, suddenly feeling very, very uncomfortable. She bit the inside of her cheek as she rocked back on her heels.

No one offered any words. Nothing. No angry tirades. No supportive gestures. Perhaps she hadn't thought this whole thing through.

Too late to change her mind now. Riley pushed her shoulders back and faced the firing squad, er, her fellow townsfolk.

"You're the Bayside Blogger?" someone asked.

"Yes. I am." She wanted to say more, to offer some kind of explanation, but a muffle in the crowd caught her attention.

Claudia was elbowing her way to the front of the stage.

When she reached it, she turned back. "That's not true, either. I'm the Bayside Blogger. I'm the one who's been writing all those blogs and social media posts."

Whispering began in the audience as Riley started stuttering. "Wait, no..."

"So am I. I'm the Bayside Blogger."

Everyone turned to see another member of the *Bugle* staff who was standing near the closest bar. He raised his glass in salute and took a long chug. "I've been following all of you. I get tips every day."

"No, no, no. You guys don't have to..." Riley tried again, but no one was paying her any attention. No one except Sawyer, who sidled up to her and grabbed her hand.

She whirled to face him. "Why are they doing this? They don't have to help."

"They want to," he said kindly. "So let them, Riley."

"They're all lying," Carissa called from the back of the room. With Jasper's help, she climbed up onto a chair. "I am the Bayside Blogger."

"No, you're not. You weren't even in town when it started," Simone Graves called out, annoyance in her voice. "I am the blogger."

"Wrong again," Elle said, joining Riley and Sawyer onstage. Every head in the place swiveled toward her. "It's me. I've been doing it this whole time. Even when I was in Italy. I just utilized the internet."

"Oh, please. Everyone knows I like to blog and I've been gossiping about all of you for years."

Riley couldn't keep her mouth from falling open at this latest admission from Elle's father, Ted Owens. Mr. Owens rarely even attended a Dumont event, let alone talked when he did.

Still, she couldn't believe what she was witnessing.

Every person was defending her. Or did they even realize she was the one telling the truth?

"Sawyer, are they covering for me?"

He leaned close, his breath a whisper on her neck. "I don't think they even realize that you're the real blogger. I don't think they care."

Elle put an arm around her waist. "They're protecting this town, Ri. And you're an important part of this place."

At that moment, Cam stepped onto the stage and opened his arms wide. "Now, now, I can't have my fiancée and soon-to-be father-in-law lying on my behalf. Time for me to man up."

Riley almost choked. Cam Dumont was one of the most masculine men she'd ever met and probably the least likely to even have a Facebook account, let alone know how to write a gossip column.

"I am the Bayside Blogger," he called out.

People couldn't contain their amusement at this admission. Whistles and catcalls echoed throughout the space. Cam took a bow and snagged Elle for a long, dramatic kiss.

"He must have had a few drinks. I've never seen Cam act so gregariously." Sawyer grinned.

"This night keeps getting more surprising by the second," Riley said.

"Sometimes I'm the Bayside Blogger."

Everyone stopped talking and turned toward Mrs. Dumont. She flung back her head and leveled a bold stare at the crowd. No one dared contradict Lilah Dumont.

"Hey, I've tipped the blogger off more than once," admitted Tony from The Brewside from the middle of the room. "Guess that makes me the blogger, too."

"You've tipped off the Bayside Blogger?" Jasper asked with shock in his voice.

"Hey, I work in the heart of the town. I know all the good gossip."

"Dude," Jasper said with a smirk and a head shake.

Dan tapped his finger against the microphone. Apparently he was done with this charade. "Who is really the Bayside Blogger? I demand to know."

"We all are."

"The Bayside Blogger is part of our town. And our town sticks together. So don't think you can come in here and try to rip us apart."

Riley wasn't even sure who was saying what at this point. Tears threatened her eyes. She was beyond moved at the loyalty of Bayside.

Mrs. Dumont moved to the center of the stage and reached her arm out. Dan immediately handed over the microphone. "I believe you have your answer, Mr. Melwood. Now, we are going to continue celebrating the *Bugle* tonight. You are welcome to join us or you are free to leave. Your choice."

With an expression of defeat, Dan slumped off stage and made his way to the nearest exit, shaking his head. A loud round of applause roared through the crowd.

"Now, Bayside," Mrs. Dumont corrected them. "Let's keep it classy." But she was grinning from ear to ear as she said it.

It definitely took some time, but eventually talk of Dan Melwood, the Bayside Blogger and the very exciting start to this party died down.

"Wow, just wow," Carissa said as she and Jasper found Riley and Sawyer.

"Tell me about it," Riley agreed.

Cam and Elle made their way over with champagne for everyone. Well, everyone but Carissa, who enjoyed a large ginger ale in a champagne flute.

"I just love this town," Elle said.

Riley had to hold in a smirk. She remembered not too long ago when Elle was ready to pull her hair out at the thought of staying in Bayside. Of course, Riley may have been responsible for that attitude since the Bayside Blogger had kinda, sorta made it difficult for her. But in the end, Elle and Cam fell in love, so the end justified the means.

Riley took a moment to glance around at the party. The band was playing. People were dancing. Guests were enjoying the drinks and the food.

And she and Sawyer were in love.

Everything was perfect.

"Tell me about the *Bugle*'s financial troubles," Jasper said to Sawyer.

Well, almost perfect. For a few minutes there, Riley had allowed herself to forget that there was still one very big problem. The fate of the newspaper hung in the air.

Sawyer must have allowed himself a brief reprieve from his worries, too, because at Jasper's question his face fell. The smile he'd been wearing slipped away and his eyes narrowed.

But he explained what was happening with publishing and specifically with the *Bugle* to Jasper. Riley couldn't help noticing that Elle, Carissa and Cam were all listening attentively, too.

It was bad. The newspaper needed help.

She'd never seen Jasper in business mode before. The usually charming and fun-loving Dumont brother had become serious while he took in every word from the editor. His arms were crossed over his chest. He didn't ask any questions, only occasionally nodded.

When Sawyer finished, Jasper responded. "What I'd like to know is, why didn't you come to me sooner?"

Sawyer appeared to blush. "Honestly, I did think of your family. But you're in real estate. I didn't think you'd be interested in signing on to the publishing world." He rocked back on his heels and scrubbed a hand over his face. "Although, you are opening that bookstore on the other side of town."

Jasper raised an eyebrow.

"It's official. I'm an idiot," Sawyer said, as he worked through everything out loud.

Jasper chuckled. "Come with me."

Carissa placed a hand on Riley's arm when she wanted to follow the two of them. Carissa smiled and shook her head. "Let them talk."

"But…" Riley protested.

"But nothing. I filled Jasper in on all of this last night after you told me and Elle what was going on. He was up all night on his computer. I think he has the solution to two problems."

That was great. Then something dawned on her. "Two problems? What's the second?"

Carissa remained tight-lipped. After what felt like an eternity, Sawyer and Jasper returned, wearing matching grins.

Riley jumped in front of Sawyer. "What happened?"

"Meet my new silent partner. Mr. Jasper Dumont has agreed to work with me to keep the *Bugle* going," Sawyer announced.

Riley let out a long, relieved sigh. It felt like the weight of the world had just lessened. She couldn't even imagine how Sawyer felt although, the way his eyes were shining, she had a pretty good idea.

"We have some details to work out, but I think that can wait until Monday." Jasper stuck his hand out and

Sawyer didn't waste time shaking it. "I couldn't be happier to help such a worthy institution."

Carissa crossed to her boyfriend and wound an arm around his waist. "What about the other thing, Jasp?"

"Ah, yes." Jasper placed a kiss on the top of her head. "I probably shouldn't do this in such a public forum, but since we're all friends and tonight is a celebration, why not." He faced Riley. "As you all know, I'm opening a bookstore."

"How's that going?" Elle asked.

"Everything is right on schedule, except for one tiny thing. I don't have a manager. There's a certain type of person I'm looking for and I've yet to find her." He continued staring at Riley.

Did he think she knew someone to manage a bookstore? In all honesty, she couldn't wait for the Bookworm to open and planned to spend a lot of time there. How fun to have a place that would sell new and used books. Bayside really needed someplace small and local that catered to the community and—

"Ri," Sawyer said, amusement in his voice.

"What?" She realized that Jasper wasn't the only person watching her. Everyone in the group had turned their attention in her direction. "What?" she repeated.

Jasper cleared his throat. "I was wondering if you had any interest in applying for the manager position?"

"Me? You're kidding."

Jasper shook his head. "Nope. I need someone who is good with people, who knows the town, who likes reading. I want someone who not only knows books but understands social media and more current forms of communication. I think you might just be that person."

Riley was stunned. She clasped Sawyer's arm in excitement. "Ohmigod. Jasper, this is amazing! Of course I'm interested! I'm thrilled that you'd even consider me."

"I may have told him you recently resigned from the *Bugle*," Sawyer added.

"Let's have lunch this week and talk it over," Jasper said.

In the matter of a few hours, everything seemed to go from dark to light. Dan Melwood's threat was gone, the *Bugle* was saved, and she might have a new career to look forward to.

Then there was Sawyer.

As their friends dispersed to enjoy the party, Sawyer reached for her hand. He led her to the middle of the dance floor and swept her into his arms.

She'd never felt more at home.

"Happy?" he asked.

"Beyond words," she replied. "I'm just so ecstatic the way everything has turned out."

"Me, too," Sawyer said. "Plus, I've made a decision. I'm going to take some advice a good friend offered me."

Riley cocked her head.

"My favorite redhead suggested I learn to evolve. I think she was right."

"She sounds really wise. And beautiful."

"She's both." Sawyer kissed her. "We're going to stop printing the *Bugle* every day of the week. We're going down to three times a week plus a Sunday edition. Some special editions throughout the year."

She knew that decision must have been hard for him. At first, it would have made him feel like a failure. But she knew it was the right way to go and she couldn't be prouder that he'd come around to it.

"You're going to have some extra time on your hands."

Her arms tightened around his neck. "However will you fill it?"

Sawyer met her gaze. "I'm going to be spending it with my new fiancée."

Oh. Oh? *Oh!*

Her hands started shaking as she backed up from him. "What did you just say?"

"Hmm," he said lazily. "I thought you heard me but I guess not. So let me make it crystal clear."

Sawyer got down on one knee right in the middle of the dance floor. People stopped dancing and faced them. She thought she saw phones being held up to capture the moment, but she couldn't tear her eyes from Sawyer. Especially when he pulled something out from his back pocket and she realized it was a ring box.

"Ohmigod," she exclaimed, her hands flying to her mouth. She was so caught off guard that she barely noticed everyone in the tent was sighing and gasping.

"Now you're sounding more like yourself. And you know what? I love who you are, Riley Hudson. I love how obsessed you are with *The Real Housewives*, but that you read *Newsweek* while you watch them. I love that you never miss an episode of *Entertainment Tonight*. I love that you're the Bayside Blogger," he whispered. "I love that behind all those outrageous outfits you parade around in, you have the biggest heart on the planet. I love how well you know me and how you've always been there for me."

Sawyer coughed.

"I love you, Riley."

She leaned over and kissed him. "And I love you, Sawyer Wallace."

"Marry me?" he asked.

She couldn't stop the smile from blossoming if she'd tried. "Of course."

Sawyer twirled her around until she was dizzy. Or maybe that was from being so in love and so happy.

The crowd applauded wildly and Sawyer grinned.

"Wait, wait," she said, fumbling in her tiny purse. "We have to snap a selfie." She turned to him. "You're not going to get away with being camera shy this time, Mr. Editor in Chief."

As she held her phone up, Sawyer leaned in, wrapped his arms around her and smiled—for real. They took a whole round of selfies showing off her new ring, their matching smiles, and the love that had been steadily growing between them since they were kids. Even as a brand-new bride-to-be, Riley couldn't help imagining the headlines her own engagement could make for her column! Not that she'd ever write about herself again…

Then Sawyer yelled out, "Can someone make sure to tip off the Bayside Blogger about this?"

Riley laughed as her phone vibrated, the tips no doubt pouring in. Finally, the blogger would have the scoop she'd been waiting on for a long, long time.

Epilogue

What a great start to a new year.

Smiling, Riley crossed to the window of her apartment and hip-bumped Sawyer. Her fiancé. She still couldn't believe it.

Sawyer's arm shot out and wrapped around her waist, bringing her snugly to him. The room was dark except for the pretty light emanating from her Christmas tree. Riley never took down her tree until after New Year's.

They stared out at the bay, aglow with the twinkly lights the town had put up after Thanksgiving. All of the boats were decorated, the large tree still stood in the town square, all of the stores and businesses were illuminated. Most of the town's residents were down there. She and Sawyer had been in the crowd until ten minutes ago.

They'd eaten dinner at the Boathouse with all of their friends and family. It had been one of the best nights of her life.

Tony closed The Brewside early and joined them for dinner. He joked about not having anyone to kiss at midnight, but Riley suspected there was something deeper under the laughter. Hmm, wouldn't the Bayside Blogger be all over that one, she thought with a smirk.

Jasper and Cam chastised him for giving tips to the blogger but Tony simply grinned. "I work in the eye of the gossip storm. Besides, I didn't want the blogger to get any details wrong."

More reason to love Tony. "Truth in reporting is important," Riley said.

Elle and Cam sneaked glances at each other all night. Mrs. Dumont excitedly talked about their upcoming wedding as Mr. Dumont pretended to be exasperated by his wife.

Elle's dad announced that he'd been at the doctor's that morning for one of his checkups and was still cancer-free. Everyone at the table let out a collective sigh of relief and they all toasted the wonderful news.

Riley's parents kept hugging Sawyer throughout the dinner, something they'd been doing his whole life. But tonight it had been different. It was a kind of blessing and she loved watching Sawyer blush with the attention.

Riley chatted with Sawyer's mom and dad, who couldn't believe she was leaving the *Bugle* in a couple of weeks. But Riley was excited to start her new career. She toasted Jasper and thanked him for the millionth time. She was going to run a bookstore. She could barely believe it. Plus, a new job called for a new wardrobe.

As they finished up dessert, Jasper and Carissa shared a glance. Then Jasper tapped his knife against Carissa's glass of water to get everyone's attention.

To a rapt audience, the two of them announced they were expecting the newest Dumont in seven months' time. Riley had to hold back tears as she watched everyone explode with congratulations and well wishes. If she thought Mrs. Dumont was excited to plan Cam and Elle's wedding, it was nothing compared to the idea of planning for a first grandchild.

They all left the restaurant together, strolling lazily through the town square where there would be an official countdown to the New Year followed by fireworks over the bay. But Sawyer whispered a suggestion to Riley and she couldn't agree more. He wanted to share this moment with her, and only her. Since they could see everything from her apartment, they decided to quietly slip away.

Before they did, she took a moment to hug her two best girlfriends. She and Elle teased the always-gorgeous Carissa about how excited they were she would be getting fat.

"Bitches," Carissa said with a laugh. "But, seriously, who's in for a little prenatal yoga?"

"You know I am. Some of my best conversations happen in yoga," Riley said with her best mischievous smile.

Elle grabbed both of them into a group hug. "I love you both so much. I can't believe the last year."

"It's been wonderful," Carissa agreed.

Riley peeked at Sawyer. "Feels like we're all exactly where we should be." And what a wonderful, empowering feeling that was. To be happy. To be loved. To be content. There was nothing better.

So, she left her friends, joking that she would see them next year. Then she and Sawyer made their way back to her apartment. It would be the last New Year's Eve she would live on the sixth floor of this building. They had big plans in the coming months. A summer wedding. Before that, she was going to move into Sawyer's house where they'd have more room.

She opened one of her windows so the happy sounds from below could filter up to them. The countdown began.

As for the Bayside Blogger? Well, except for one thank-you tweet to the town of Bayside, she'd been quiet this week. She might be quiet for a long time. Then again, when it came to the Bayside Blogger, who knew. She did love a good surprise.

Ten, nine, eight...

The day after the *Bugle*'s party, Riley had received a big tip to her Bayside Blogger email. A video of Sawyer proposing to her. Happily, she posted it on the website and watched it a million times as she snuggled on the couch with her lifelong friend, her soon-to-be former boss and her very amazing fiancé.

Three, two, one!

"Happy New Year, Riley."

"Happy New Year, Sawyer."

She kissed him for the first couple minutes of the New Year, happy knowing that at last she, too, had been saved by the blog.

* * * * *

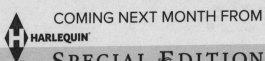

COMING NEXT MONTH FROM

HARLEQUIN®

SPECIAL EDITION

Available January 16, 2018

#2599 NO ORDINARY FORTUNE
The Fortunes of Texas: The Rulebreakers • by Judy Duarte
Carlo Mendoza always thought he had the market cornered on charm, until he met Schuyler Fortunado. She's a force of nature—and secretly a Fortune! And when Schuyler takes a job with Carlo at the Mendoza Winery, sparks fly!

#2600 A SOLDIER IN CONARD COUNTY
American Heroes • by Rachel Lee
After an injury places him on indefinite leave, Special Forces sergeant Gil York ends up in Conard County to escape his overbearing family. Miriam Baker, a gentle music teacher, senses Gil needs more than a place to stay and coaxes him out from behind his walls. But is he willing to face his past to make a future with Miriam?

#2601 AN ENGAGEMENT FOR TWO
Matchmaking Mamas • by Marie Ferrarella
The Matchmaking Mamas are at it again, this time for Mikki McKenna, a driven internist who has always shied away from commitment. But when Jeff Sabatino invites her to dine at his restaurant and sparks a chance at a relationship, she begins to wonder if this table for two might be worth the risk after all.

#2602 A BRIDE FOR LIAM BRAND
The Brands of Montana • by Joanna Sims
Kate King has settled into her role as rancher and mother, but with her daughter exploring her independence, she thinks she might want to give handsome Liam Brand a chance. But her ex and his daughter are both determined to cause trouble, and Kate and Liam will have to readjust their visions of the future to claim their own happily-ever-after.

#2603 THE SINGLE DAD'S FAMILY RECIPE
The McKinnels of Jewell Rock • by Rachael Johns
Single-dad chef Lachlan McKinnell is opening a restaurant at his family's whiskey distillery and struggling to find a suitable head hostess. Trying to recover from tragedy, Eliza Coleman thinks a move to Jewell Rock and a job at a brand-new restaurant could be the fresh start she's looking for. She never expected to fall for her boss, but it's beginning to look like they have all the ingredients for a perfect family!

#2604 THE MARINE'S SECRET DAUGHTER
Small-Town Sweethearts • by Carrie Nichols
When he returns to his hometown, marine Riley Cooper finds the girl he left behind living next door. But there's more between them than the heartbreak they gave each other—and five-year-old Fiona throws quite a wrench in their reunion. Will Riley choose the marines and a safe heart, or will he risk it all on the family he didn't even know he had?

YOU CAN FIND MORE INFORMATION ON UPCOMING HARLEQUIN® TITLES, FREE EXCERPTS AND MORE AT WWW.HARLEQUIN.COM.

HSECNM0118

Get 2 Free Books,
Plus 2 Free Gifts—
just for trying the Reader Service!

♦ HARLEQUIN®
SPECIAL EDITION

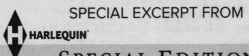
"Sorry," she said. "I just feel so helpless. Talk away. I'll keep my mouth shut."

"I don't want that." Then he caused her to catch her breath by sliding down the couch until he was right beside her. He slipped his arm around her shoulders, and despite her surprise, it seemed the most natural thing in the world to lean into him and finally let her head come to rest on his shoulder.

"Holding you is nice," he said quietly. "You quiet the rat race in my head. Does that sound awful?"

How could it? she wondered, when she'd been amazed at the way he had caused her to melt, as if everything else went away and she was in a warm, soft, safe space. If she could offer him any part of that, she would, gladly.

"If that sounds like I'm using you…"

"Man, don't you ever stop? Do you ever just go with the flow?" Turning and tilting her head a bit, she pressed a quick kiss on his lips.

"What the…" He sounded surprised.

"You're analyzing constantly," she told him. "This isn't a mission. Let it go. Let go. Just relax and hold me, and I hope you're enjoying it as much as I am."

Because she was. That wonderful melting filled her again, leaving her soft and very, very content. Maybe even happy.

"You are?" he murmured.

"I am. More than I've ever enjoyed a hug." God, had she ever been this blunt with a man before? But this guy was so bound up behind his walls and drawbridges, she wondered if she'd need a sledgehammer to get through.

But then she remembered Al and the distance she'd sensed in him during his visits. Not exactly alone, but alone among family. These guys had been deeply changed by their training and experience. Where did they find comfort now? Real comfort?

Her thoughts were slipping away in response to a growing anticipation and anxiety. She was close, so close to him, and his strength drew her like a bee to nectar. He even smelled good, still carrying the scents from the storm outside and his earlier shower, but beneath that the aroma of male.

Everything inside her became focused on one trembling hope, that he'd take this hug further, that he'd draw her closer and begin to explore her with his hands and mouth.

Don't miss
A SOLDIER IN CONARD COUNTY by Rachel Lee,
available February 2018 wherever
Harlequin® Special Edition books and ebooks are sold.

www.Harlequin.com

HSEEXP0118

Looking for more satisfying love stories
with community and family at their core?

Check out **Harlequin® Special Edition**
and **Harlequin® Western Romance** books!

New books available every month!

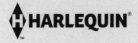

LOVE
Harlequin
romance?

Join our Harlequin community to share your thoughts and connect with other romance readers!

Be the first to find out about promotions, news, and exclusive content!

Sign up for the Harlequin e-newsletter and download a free book from any series at

www.TryHarlequin.com

CONNECT WITH US AT:

Harlequin.com/Community

 Facebook.com/HarlequinBooks

 Twitter.com/HarlequinBooks

 Instagram.com/HarlequinBooks

 Pinterest.com/HarlequinBooks

ReaderService.com

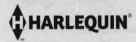

**ROMANCE WHEN
YOU NEED IT**

HSOCIAL2017